Disney

DUMBO

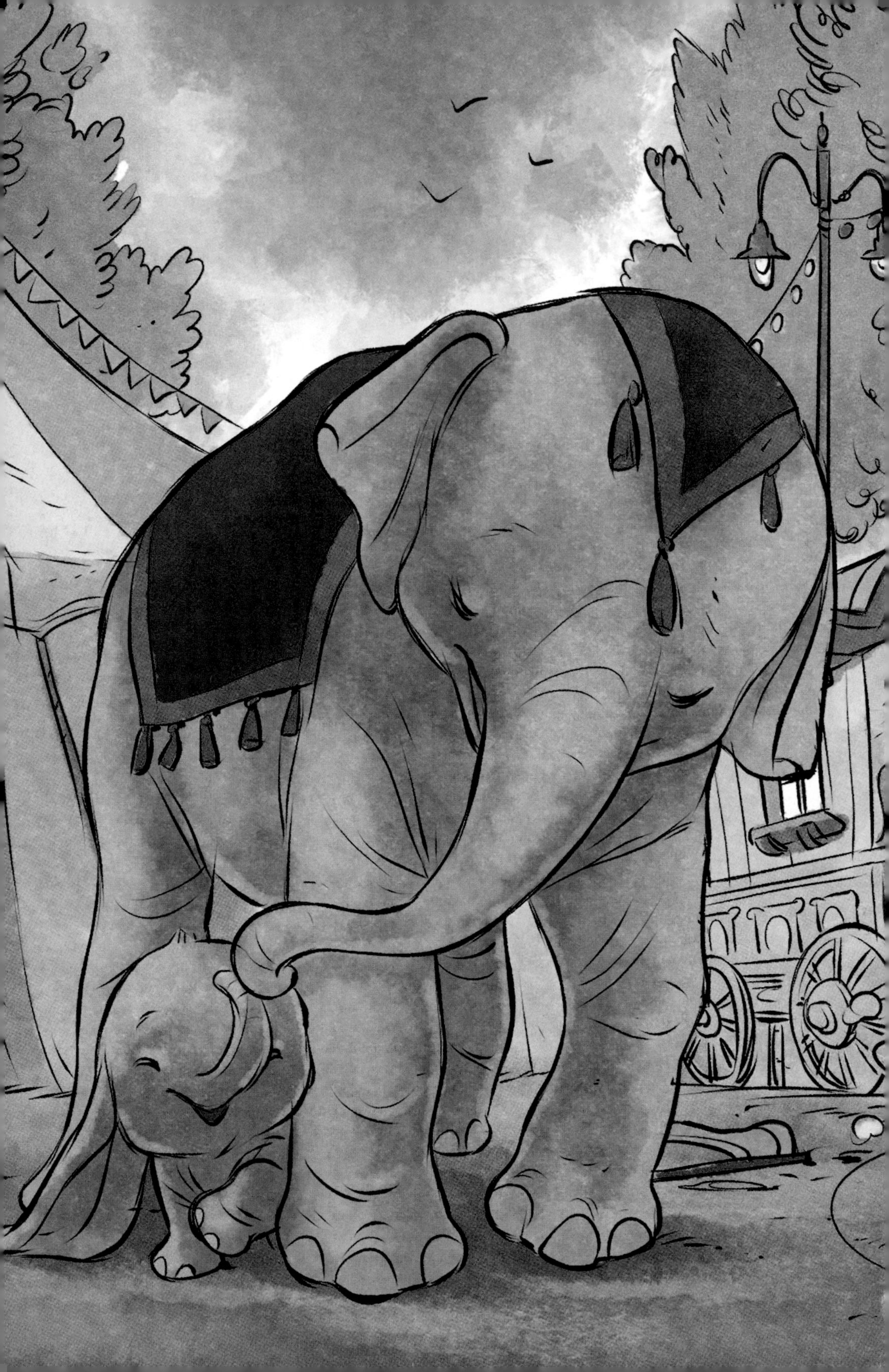

DUMBO

FRIENDS IN HIGH PLACES

Script
JOHN JACKSON MILLER

Art
ANNA MERLI with **GIUSEPPE DI MAIO**
GIOVANNI RIGANO
ALBERTO ZANON
ROSA LA BARBERA
PAOLA ANTISTA

Colors
TOMATOFARM COLOR TEAM

Lettering
RICHARD STARKINGS and
COMICRAFT'S JIMMY BETANCOURT

Cover Art
GIOVANNI RIGANO with
TOMATOFARM COLOR TEAM

Dark Horse Books

DARK HORSE BOOKS

president and publisher
MIKE RICHARDSON

editor
FREDDYE MILLER

assistant editor
JUDY KHUU

designer
DAVID NESTELLE

digital art technician
CHRISTIANNE GILLENARDO-GOUDREAU

Neil Hankerson Executive Vice President • Tom Weddle Chief Financial Officer • Randy Stradley Vice President
of Publishing • Nick McWhorter Chief Business Development Officer • Dale LaFountain Chief Information
Officer • Matt Parkinson Vice President of Marketing • Cara Niece Vice President of Production and Scheduling
• Mark Bernardi Vice President of Book Trade and Digital Sales • Ken Lizzi General Counsel • Dave Marshall
Editor in Chief • Davey Estrada Editorial Director • Chris Warner Senior Books Editor • Cary Grazzini
Director of Specialty Projects • Lia Ribacchi Art Director • Vanessa Todd-Holmes Director of Print Purchasing
• Matt Dryer Director of Digital Art and Prepress • Michael Gombos Director of International Publishing and
Licensing • Kari Yadro Director of Custom Programs • Kari Torson Director of International Licensing

DISNEY PUBLISHING WORLDWIDE GLOBAL MAGAZINES, COMICS AND PARTWORKS

PUBLISHER Lynn Waggoner • EDITORIAL TEAM Bianca Coletti (Director, Magazines), Guido Frazzini (Director, Comics),
Carlotta Quattrocolo (Executive Editor), Stefano Ambrosio (Executive Editor, New IP), Camilla Vedove (Senior Manager,
Editorial Development), Behnoosh Khalili (Senior Editor), Julie Dorris (Senior Editor), Mina Riazi (Assistant Editor),
Jonathan Manning (Assistant Editor) • DESIGN Enrico Soave (Senior Designer) • ART Ken Shue (VP, Global Art),
Manny Mederos (Senior Illustration Manager, Comics and Magazines), Roberto Santillo (Creative Director), Marco
Ghiglione (Creative Manager), Stefano Attardi (Computer Art Designer) • PORTFOLIO MANAGEMENT Olivia Ciancarelli
(Director) • BUSINESS & MARKETING Mariantonietta Galla (Marketing Manager), Virpi Korhonen (Editorial Manager)

"See the Amazing Dumbo the Flying Elephant!" line art by Anna Merli with Giuseppe di Maio
"Max Medici and the Keys to the City!" line art by Giovanni Rigano
"Ivan the Wonderful and the Magic of Science!" line art by Alberto Zanon
"Colette the Queen of the Heavens in To Catch a Cat!" line art by Rosa La Barbera
"Mrs. Jumbo and Dear Baby Dumbo and the First Lesson!" line art by Paola Antista

Disney Dumbo: Friends in High Places

Published by Dark Horse Books
A division of Dark Horse Comics LLC
10956 SE Main Street
Milwaukie, OR 97222

DarkHorse.com

To find a comics shop in your area, visit comicshoplocator.com

First edition: March 2019
ISBN 978-1-50671-268-0
Digital ISBN 978-1-50671-285-7

1 3 5 7 9 10 8 6 4 2
Printed in the United States of America

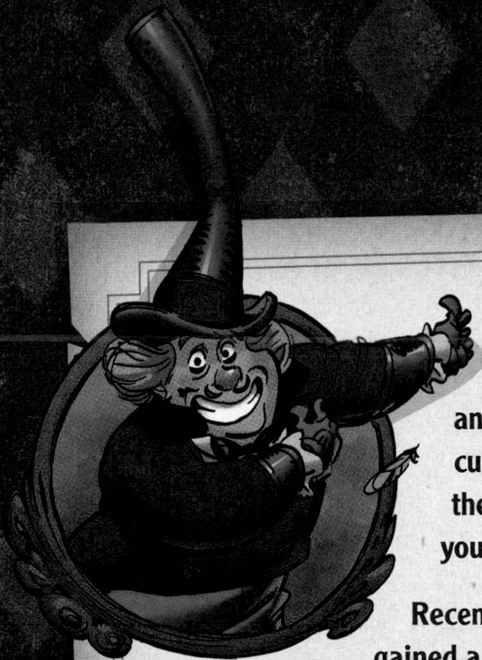

STEP RIGHT UP

to the Medici Brothers Circus and marvel at the wonders, curiosities, and possibilities as they present themselves before your eyes!

Recently, the struggling circus gained a new family member in the form of a baby elephant with oversized ears, Dumbo; and the circus owner, Max Medici, was thrilled to have this crowd-pleasing addition to the entertainment.

Soon after Dumbo joined the circus family, his caregiver's children, Milly and Joe Farrier, discovered that this peculiar pachyderm . . . *can fly*!

Now, word of Dumbo's amazing ability is spreading, he is bringing crowds to the big top, and he is intertwining with the lives of *all* the Medici Brothers Circus performers.

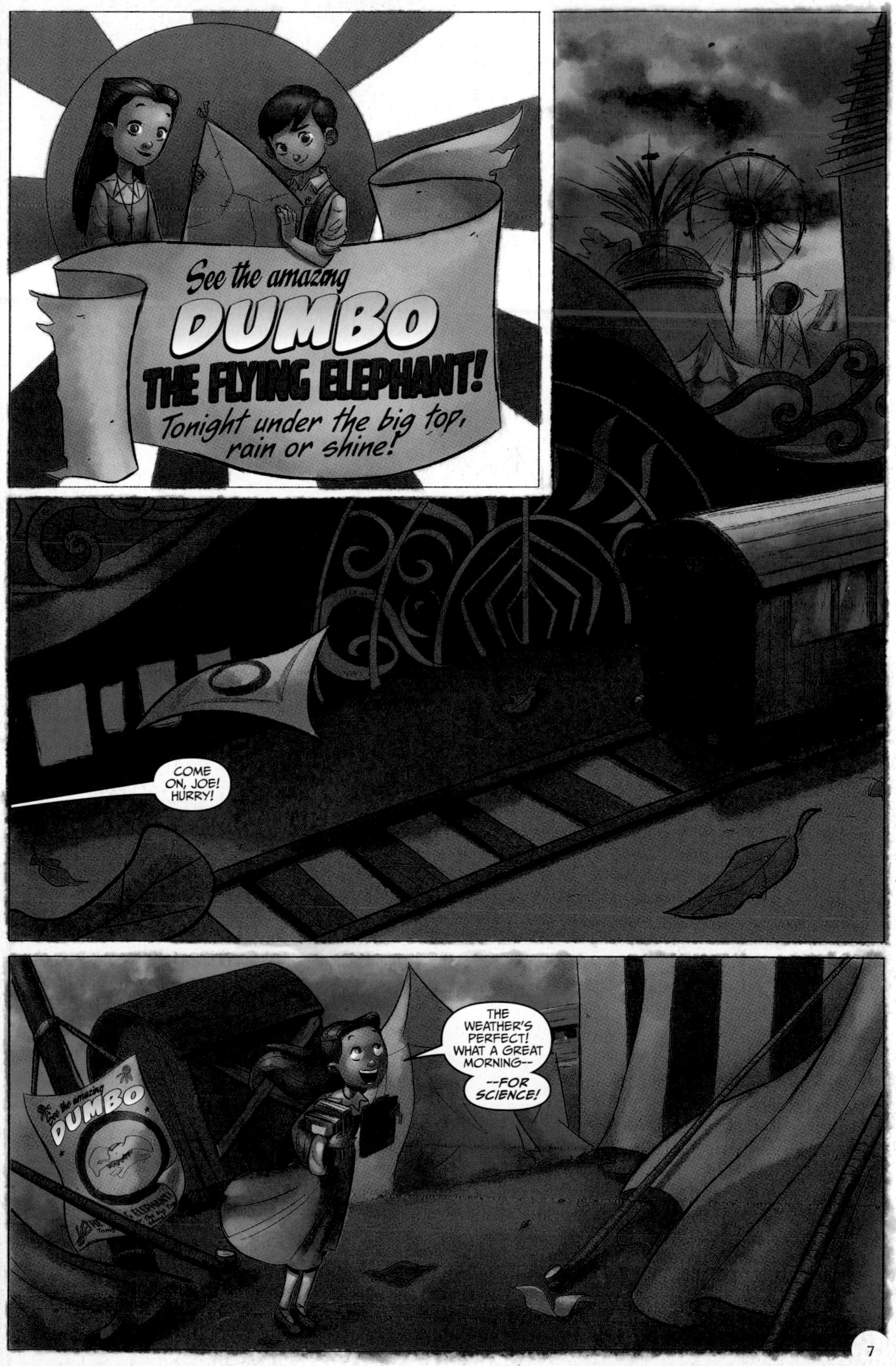
See the amazing
DUMBO
THE FLYING ELEPHANT!
Tonight under the big top, rain or shine!
COME ON, JOE! HURRY!
THE WEATHER'S PERFECT! WHAT A GREAT MORNING--
--FOR SCIENCE!
See the amazing DUMBO

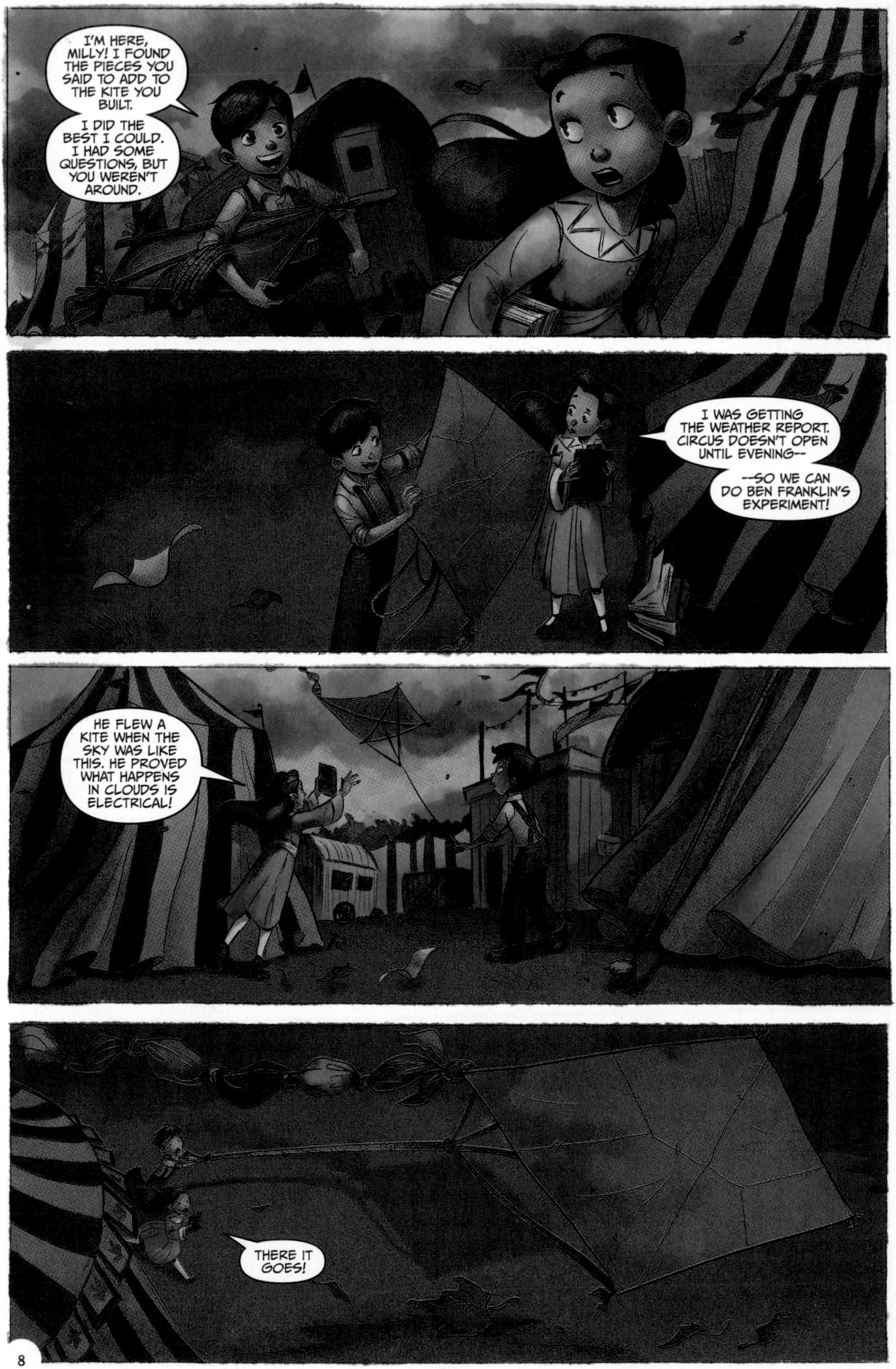
I'M HERE, MILLY! I FOUND THE PIECES YOU SAID TO ADD TO THE KITE YOU BUILT.
I DID THE BEST I COULD. I HAD SOME QUESTIONS, BUT YOU WEREN'T AROUND.
I WAS GETTING THE WEATHER REPORT. CIRCUS DOESN'T OPEN UNTIL EVENING--
--SO WE CAN DO BEN FRANKLIN'S EXPERIMENT!
HE FLEW A KITE WHEN THE SKY WAS LIKE THIS. HE PROVED WHAT HAPPENS IN CLOUDS IS ELECTRICAL!
THERE IT GOES!

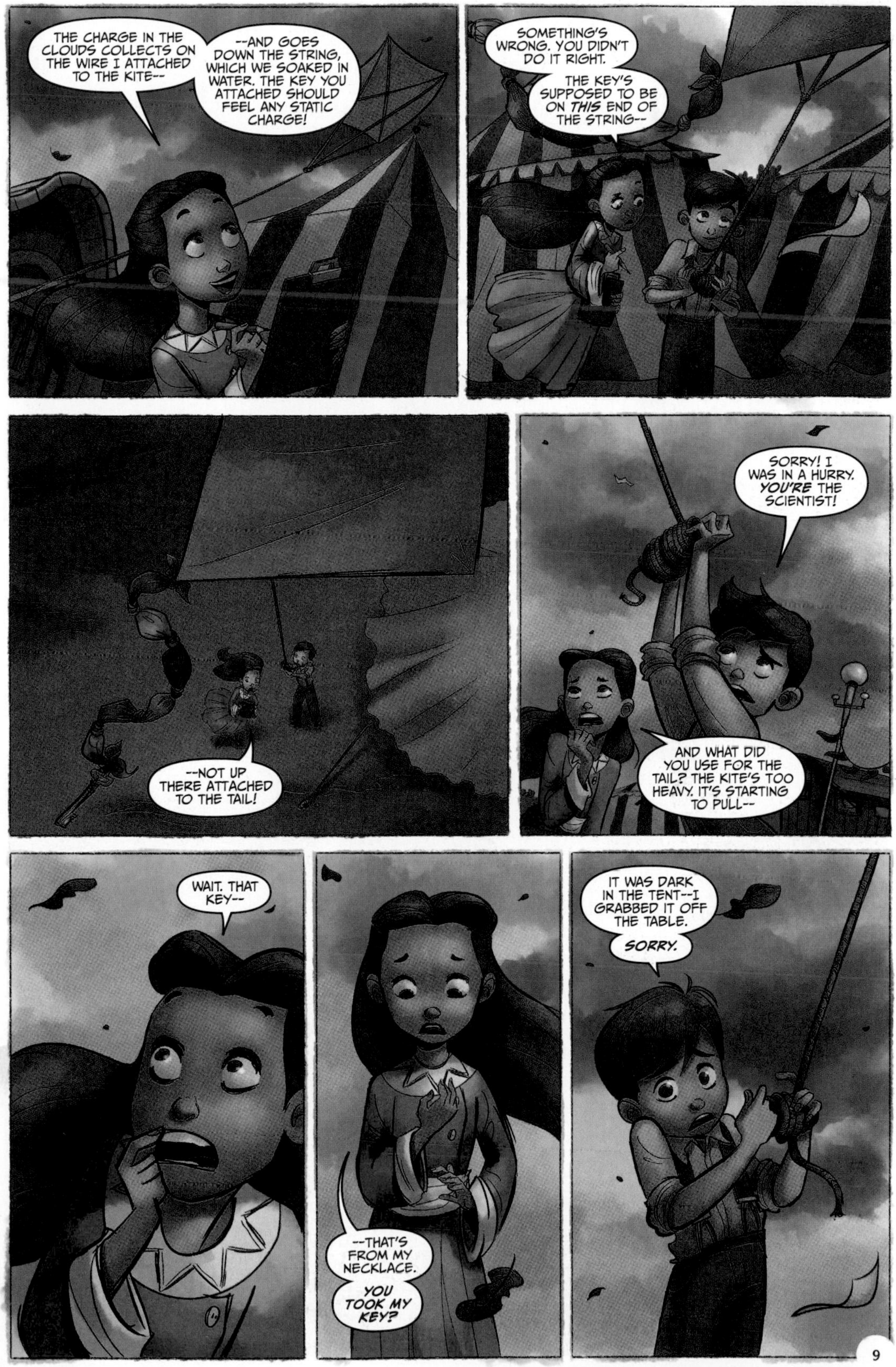
THE CHARGE IN THE CLOUDS COLLECTS ON THE WIRE I ATTACHED TO THE KITE--
--AND GOES DOWN THE STRING, WHICH WE SOAKED IN WATER. THE KEY YOU ATTACHED SHOULD FEEL ANY STATIC CHARGE!
SOMETHING'S WRONG. YOU DIDN'T DO IT RIGHT.
THE KEY'S SUPPOSED TO BE ON *THIS* END OF THE STRING--
--NOT UP THERE ATTACHED TO THE TAIL!
SORRY! I WAS IN A HURRY. *YOU'RE* THE SCIENTIST!
AND WHAT DID YOU USE FOR THE TAIL? THE KITE'S TOO HEAVY. IT'S STARTING TO PULL--
WAIT. THAT KEY--
--THAT'S FROM MY NECKLACE.
YOU TOOK MY KEY?
IT WAS DARK IN THE TENT--I GRABBED IT OFF THE TABLE.
SORRY.

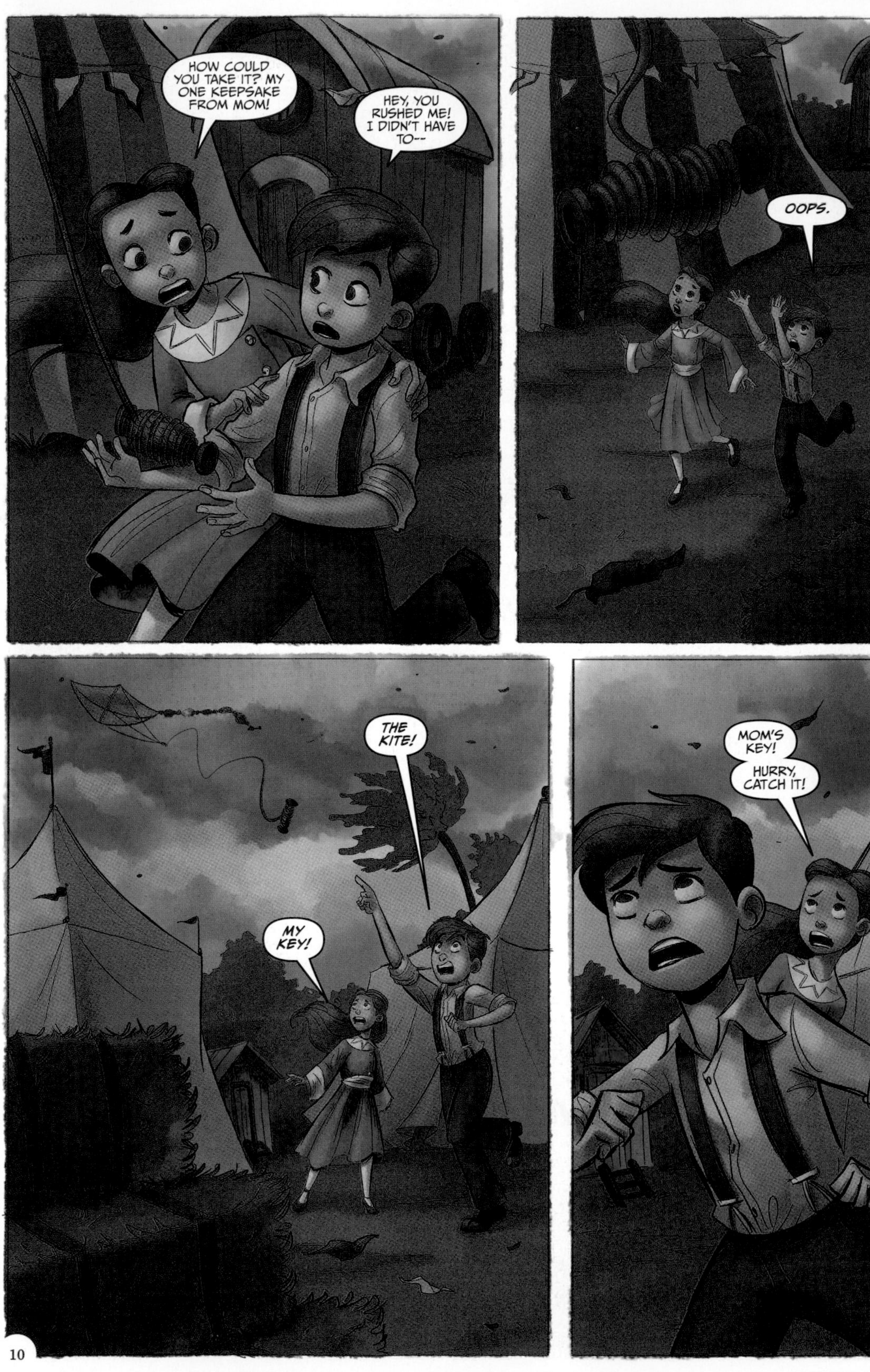
HOW COULD YOU TAKE IT? MY ONE KEEPSAKE FROM MOM!
HEY, YOU RUSHED ME! I DIDN'T HAVE TO--
OOPS.
THE KITE!
MY KEY!
MOM'S KEY!
HURRY, CATCH IT!

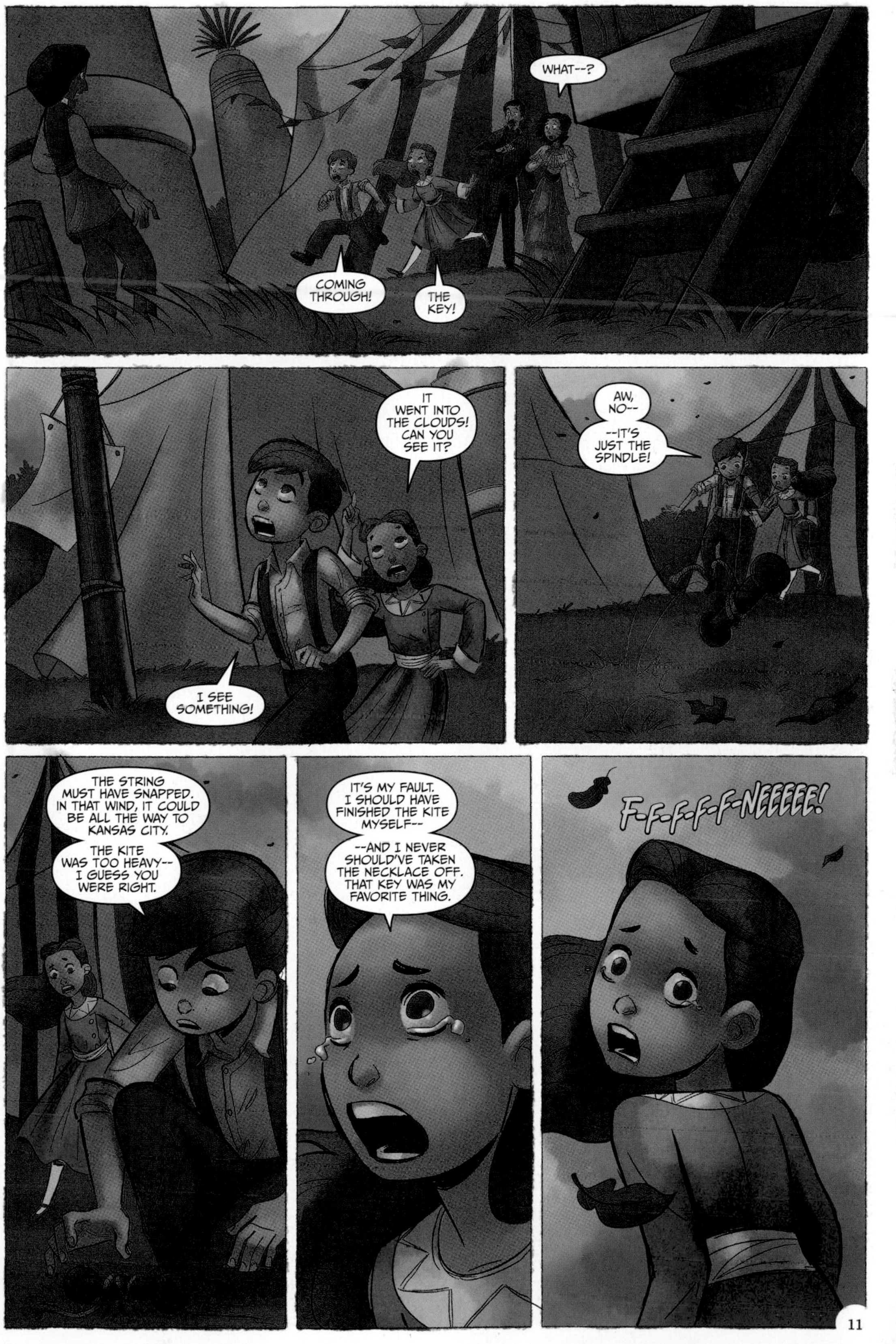
WHAT--?
COMING THROUGH!
THE KEY!
IT WENT INTO THE CLOUDS! CAN YOU SEE IT?
I SEE SOMETHING!
AW, NO--
--IT'S JUST THE SPINDLE!
THE STRING MUST HAVE SNAPPED. IN THAT WIND, IT COULD BE ALL THE WAY TO KANSAS CITY.
THE KITE WAS TOO HEAVY-- I GUESS YOU WERE RIGHT.
IT'S MY FAULT. I SHOULD HAVE FINISHED THE KITE MYSELF--
--AND I NEVER SHOULD'VE TAKEN THE NECKLACE OFF. THAT KEY WAS MY FAVORITE THING.
F-F-F-F-F-NEEEEE!

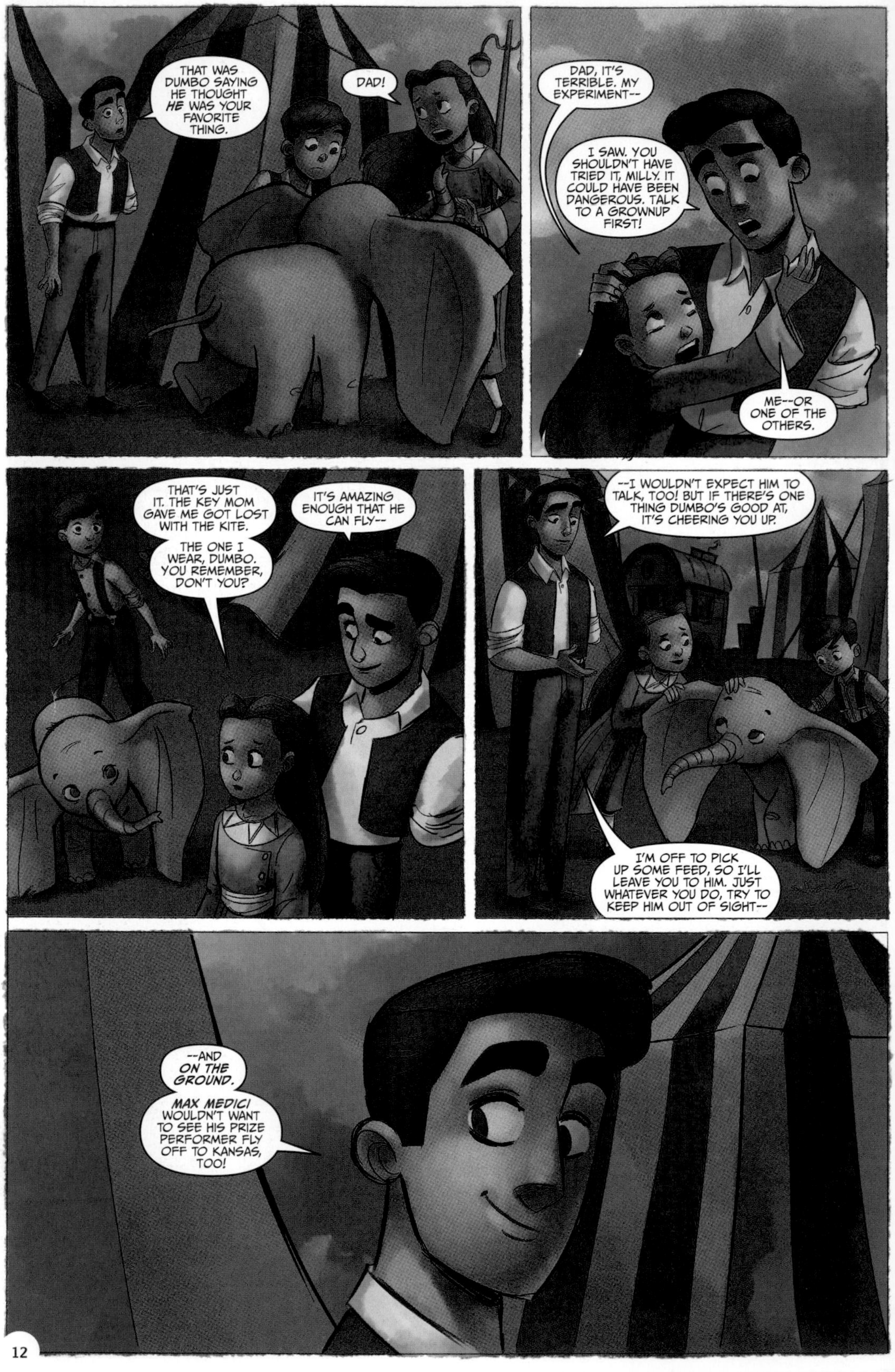
THAT WAS DUMBO SAYING HE THOUGHT *HE* WAS YOUR FAVORITE THING.
DAD!
DAD, IT'S TERRIBLE. MY EXPERIMENT--
I SAW. YOU SHOULDN'T HAVE TRIED IT, MILLY. IT COULD HAVE BEEN DANGEROUS. TALK TO A GROWNUP FIRST!
ME--OR ONE OF THE OTHERS.
THAT'S JUST IT. THE KEY MOM GAVE ME GOT LOST WITH THE KITE.
THE ONE I WEAR, DUMBO. YOU REMEMBER, DON'T YOU?
IT'S AMAZING ENOUGH THAT HE CAN FLY--
--I WOULDN'T EXPECT HIM TO TALK, TOO! BUT IF THERE'S ONE THING DUMBO'S GOOD AT, IT'S CHEERING YOU UP.
I'M OFF TO PICK UP SOME FEED, SO I'LL LEAVE YOU TO HIM. JUST WHATEVER YOU DO, TRY TO KEEP HIM OUT OF SIGHT--
--AND *ON THE GROUND*.
MAX MEDICI WOULDN'T WANT TO SEE HIS PRIZE PERFORMER FLY OFF TO KANSAS, TOO!

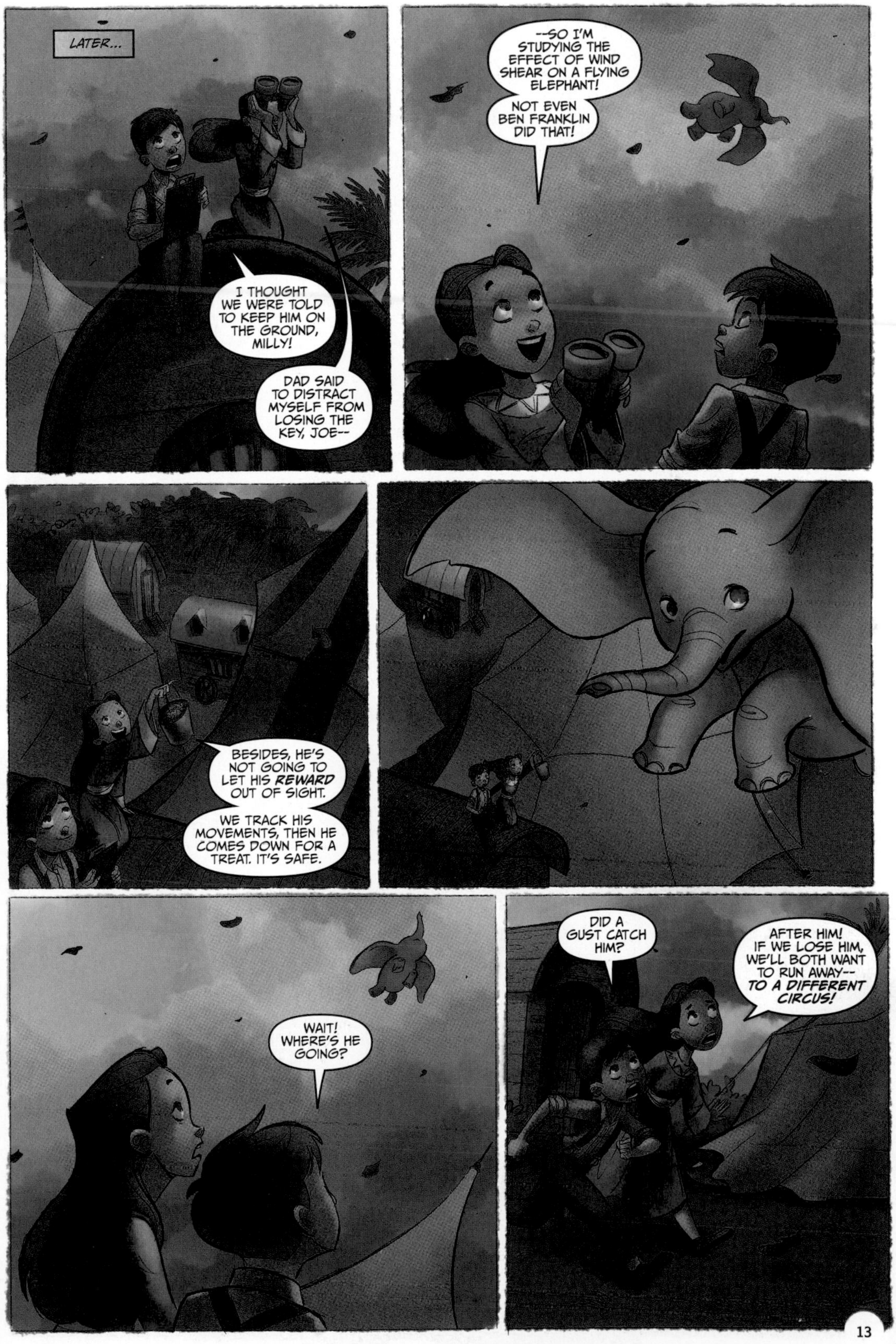
LATER...
I THOUGHT WE WERE TOLD TO KEEP HIM ON THE GROUND, MILLY!
DAD SAID TO DISTRACT MYSELF FROM LOSING THE KEY, JOE--
--SO I'M STUDYING THE EFFECT OF WIND SHEAR ON A FLYING ELEPHANT!
NOT EVEN BEN FRANKLIN DID THAT!
BESIDES, HE'S NOT GOING TO LET HIS REWARD OUT OF SIGHT.
WE TRACK HIS MOVEMENTS, THEN HE COMES DOWN FOR A TREAT. IT'S SAFE.
WAIT! WHERE'S HE GOING?
DID A GUST CATCH HIM?
AFTER HIM! IF WE LOSE HIM, WE'LL BOTH WANT TO RUN AWAY-- TO A DIFFERENT CIRCUS!

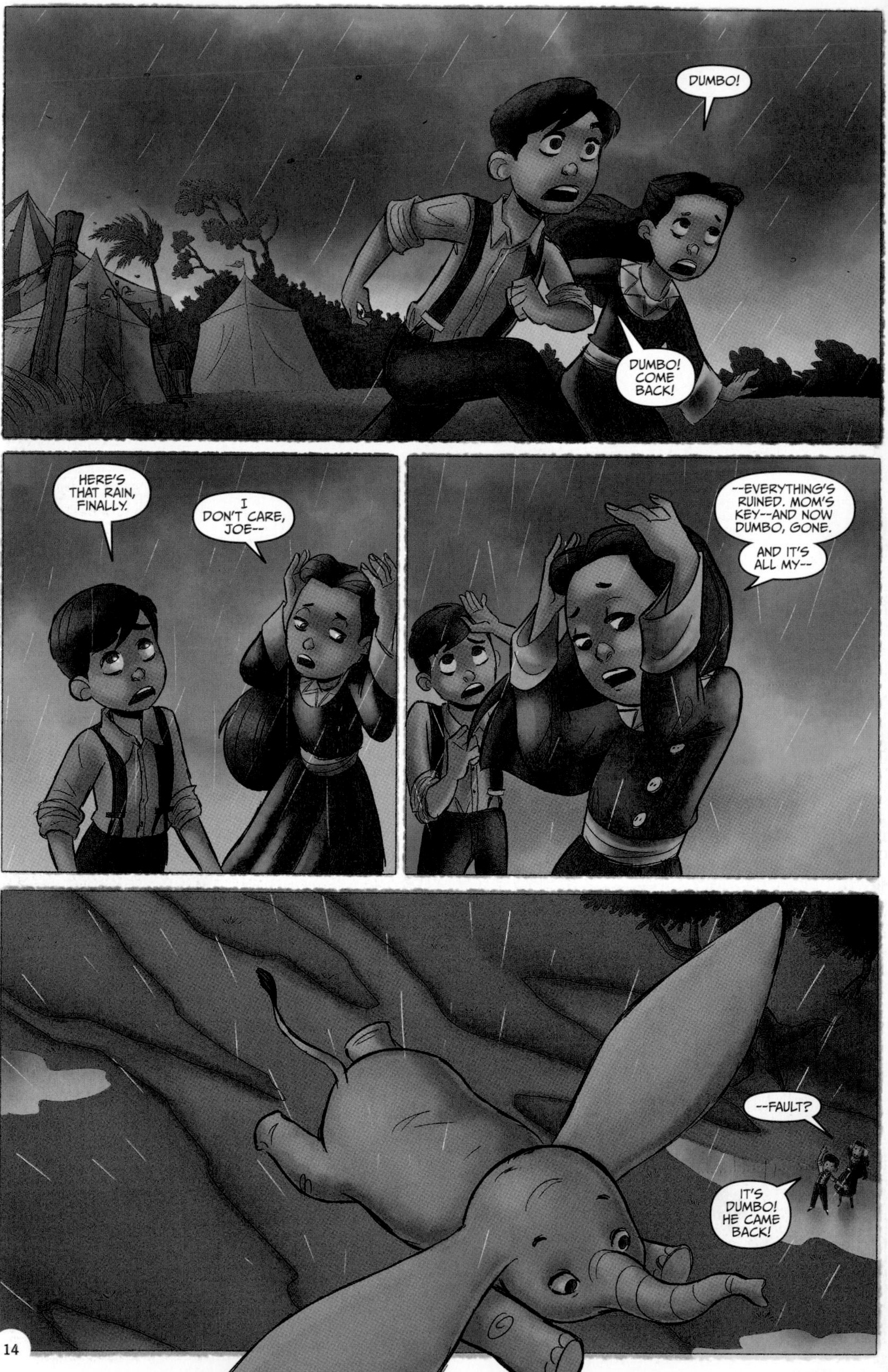
DUMBO!
DUMBO! COME BACK!
HERE'S THAT RAIN, FINALLY.
I DON'T CARE, JOE--
--EVERYTHING'S RUINED. MOM'S KEY--AND NOW DUMBO, GONE.
AND IT'S ALL MY--
--FAULT?
IT'S DUMBO! HE CAME BACK!

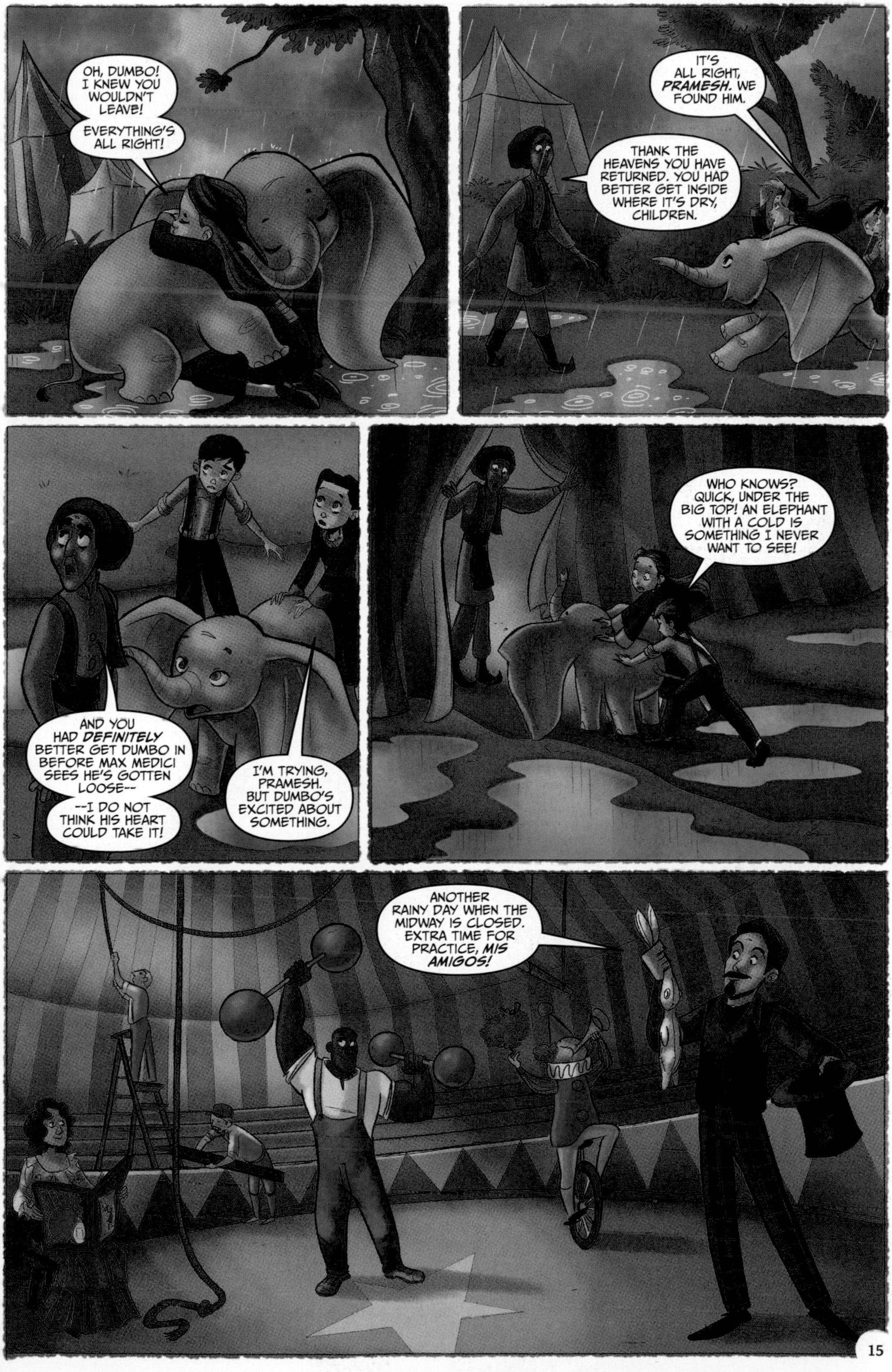
OH, DUMBO! I KNEW YOU WOULDN'T LEAVE!
EVERYTHING'S ALL RIGHT!
IT'S ALL RIGHT, PRAMESH. WE FOUND HIM.
THANK THE HEAVENS YOU HAVE RETURNED. YOU HAD BETTER GET INSIDE WHERE IT'S DRY, CHILDREN.
AND YOU HAD DEFINITELY BETTER GET DUMBO IN BEFORE MAX MEDICI SEES HE'S GOTTEN LOOSE--
--I DO NOT THINK HIS HEART COULD TAKE IT!
I'M TRYING, PRAMESH. BUT DUMBO'S EXCITED ABOUT SOMETHING.
WHO KNOWS? QUICK, UNDER THE BIG TOP! AN ELEPHANT WITH A COLD IS SOMETHING I NEVER WANT TO SEE!
ANOTHER RAINY DAY WHEN THE MIDWAY IS CLOSED. EXTRA TIME FOR PRACTICE, MIS AMIGOS!

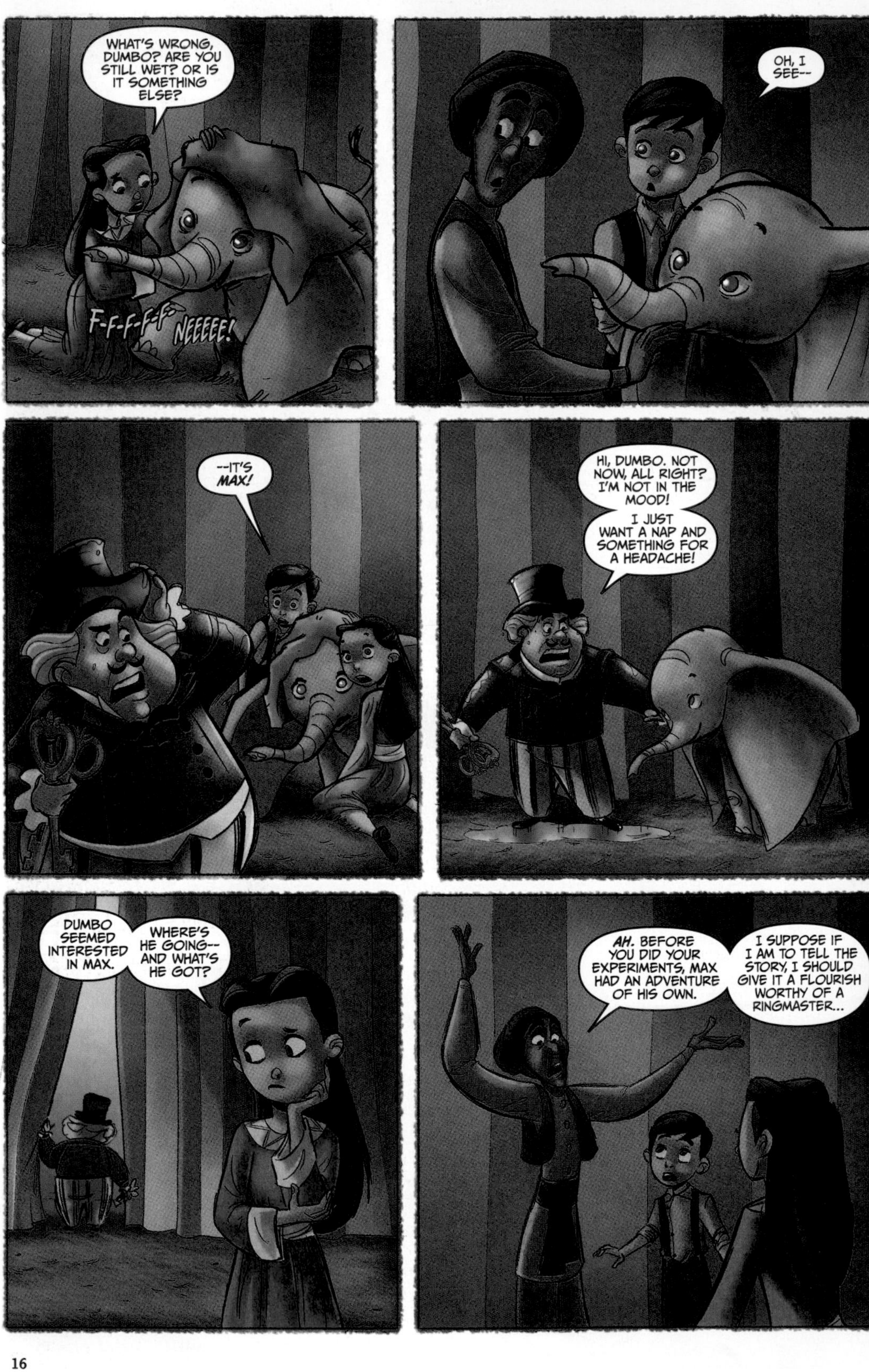
WHAT'S WRONG, DUMBO? ARE YOU STILL WET? OR IS IT SOMETHING ELSE?
F-F-F-F-F NEEEEE!
OH, I SEE--
--IT'S *MAX!*
HI, DUMBO. NOT NOW, ALL RIGHT? I'M NOT IN THE MOOD!
I JUST WANT A NAP AND SOMETHING FOR A HEADACHE!
DUMBO SEEMED INTERESTED IN MAX.
WHERE'S HE GOING--AND WHAT'S HE GOT?
AH. BEFORE YOU DID YOUR EXPERIMENTS, MAX HAD AN ADVENTURE OF HIS OWN.
I SUPPOSE IF I AM TO TELL THE STORY, I SHOULD GIVE IT A FLOURISH WORTHY OF A RINGMASTER...

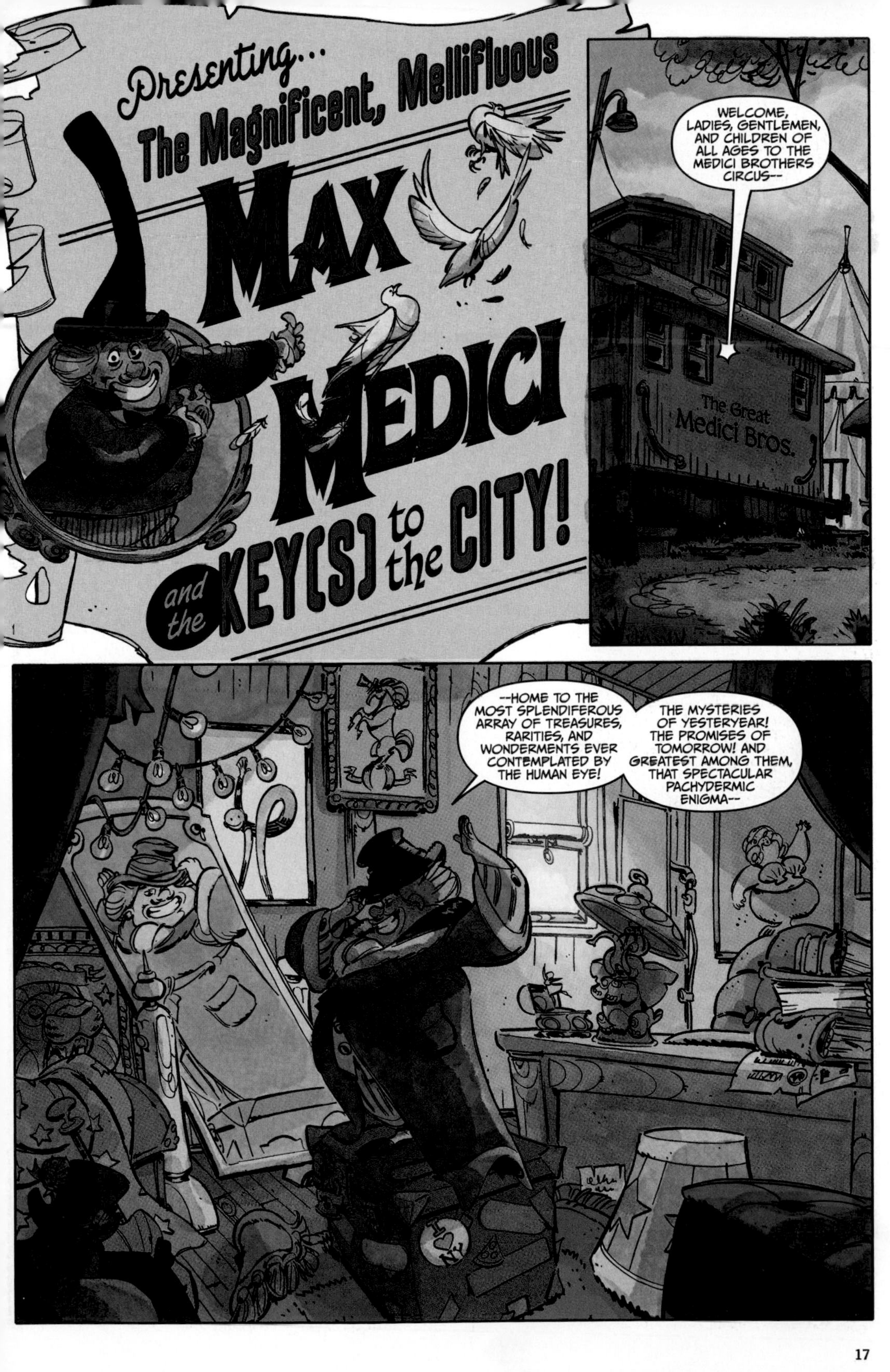
Presenting...
The Magnificent, Mellifluous
MAX MEDICI
and the KEY[S] to the CITY!
The Great Medici Bros.
WELCOME, LADIES, GENTLEMEN, AND CHILDREN OF ALL AGES TO THE MEDICI BROTHERS CIRCUS--
--HOME TO THE MOST SPLENDIFEROUS ARRAY OF TREASURES, RARITIES, AND WONDERMENTS EVER CONTEMPLATED BY THE HUMAN EYE!
THE MYSTERIES OF YESTERYEAR! THE PROMISES OF TOMORROW! AND GREATEST AMONG THEM, THAT SPECTACULAR PACHYDERMIC ENIGMA--

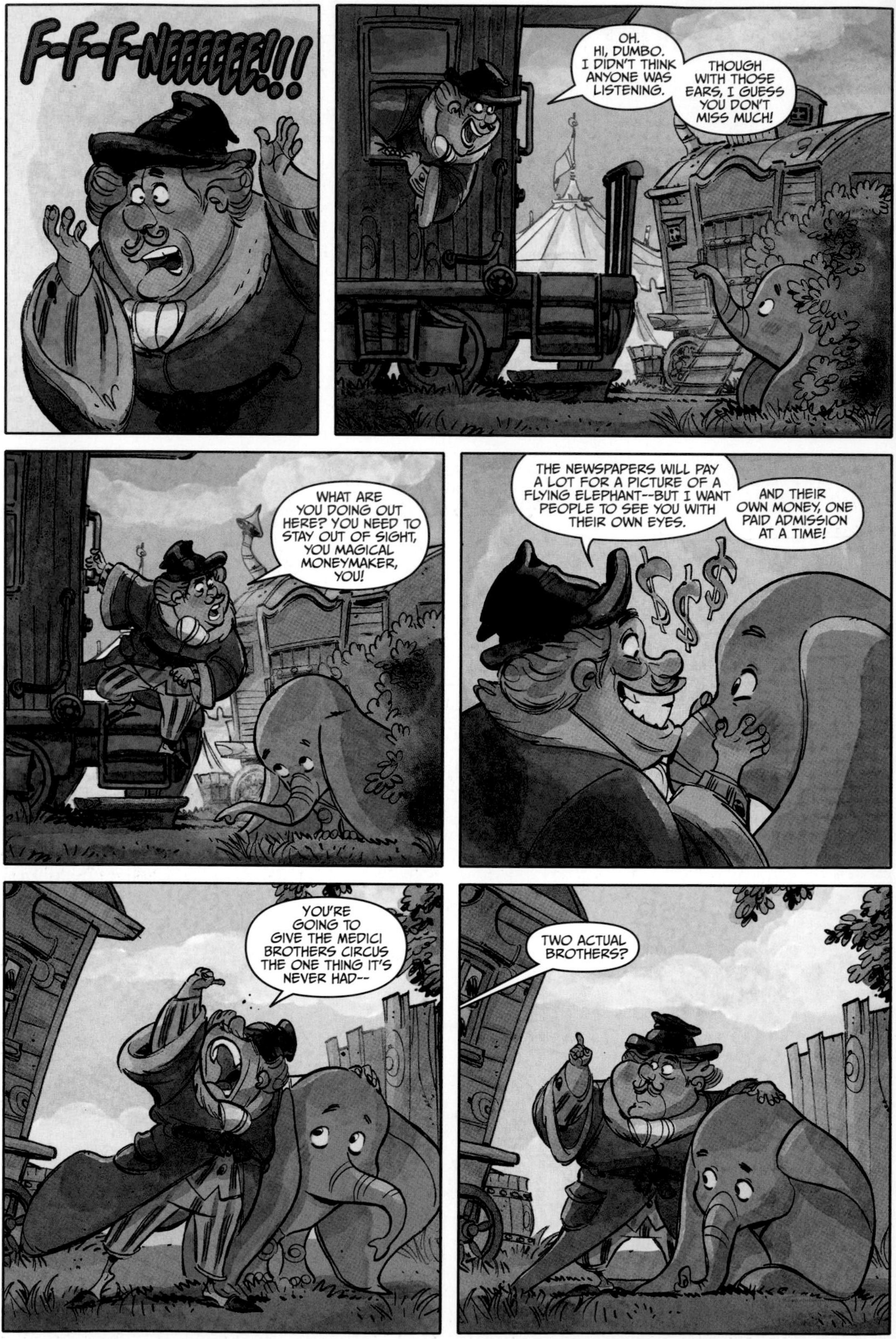
F-F-F-NEEEEEEE!!!
OH. HI, DUMBO. I DIDN'T THINK ANYONE WAS LISTENING.
THOUGH WITH THOSE EARS, I GUESS YOU DON'T MISS MUCH!
WHAT ARE YOU DOING OUT HERE? YOU NEED TO STAY OUT OF SIGHT, YOU MAGICAL MONEYMAKER, YOU!
THE NEWSPAPERS WILL PAY A LOT FOR A PICTURE OF A FLYING ELEPHANT--BUT I WANT PEOPLE TO SEE YOU WITH THEIR OWN EYES.
AND THEIR OWN MONEY, ONE PAID ADMISSION AT A TIME!
YOU'RE GOING TO GIVE THE MEDICI BROTHERS CIRCUS THE ONE THING IT'S NEVER HAD--
TWO ACTUAL BROTHERS?

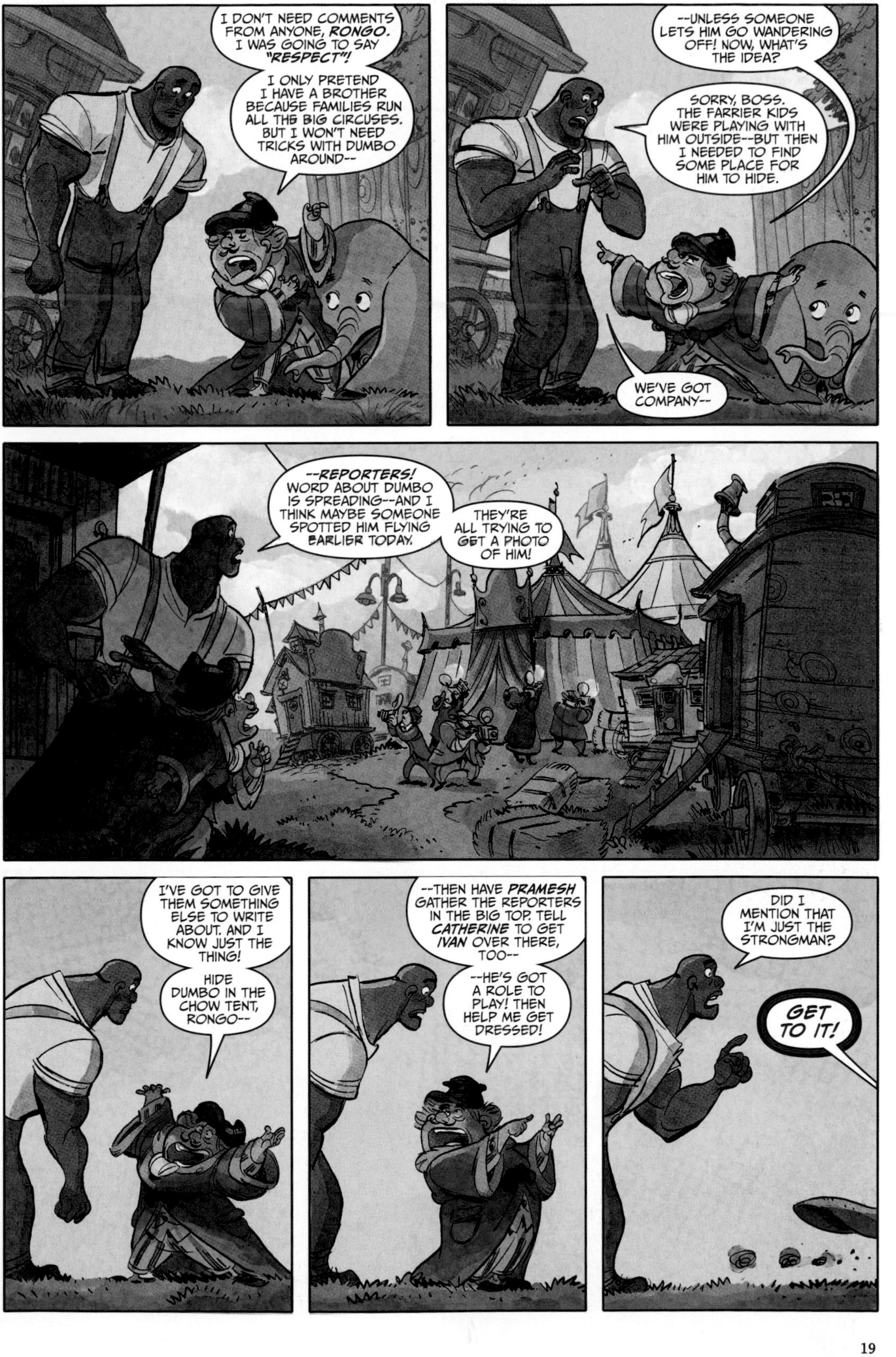
I DON'T NEED COMMENTS FROM ANYONE, RONGO. I WAS GOING TO SAY "RESPECT"!
I ONLY PRETEND I HAVE A BROTHER BECAUSE FAMILIES RUN ALL THE BIG CIRCUSES. BUT I WON'T NEED TRICKS WITH DUMBO AROUND--
--UNLESS SOMEONE LETS HIM GO WANDERING OFF! NOW, WHAT'S THE IDEA?
SORRY, BOSS. THE FARRIER KIDS WERE PLAYING WITH HIM OUTSIDE--BUT THEN I NEEDED TO FIND SOME PLACE FOR HIM TO HIDE.
WE'VE GOT COMPANY--
--REPORTERS! WORD ABOUT DUMBO IS SPREADING--AND I THINK MAYBE SOMEONE SPOTTED HIM FLYING EARLIER TODAY.
THEY'RE ALL TRYING TO GET A PHOTO OF HIM!
I'VE GOT TO GIVE THEM SOMETHING ELSE TO WRITE ABOUT. AND I KNOW JUST THE THING!
HIDE DUMBO IN THE CHOW TENT, RONGO--
--THEN HAVE PRAMESH GATHER THE REPORTERS IN THE BIG TOP. TELL CATHERINE TO GET IVAN OVER THERE, TOO--
--HE'S GOT A ROLE TO PLAY! THEN HELP ME GET DRESSED!
DID I MENTION THAT I'M JUST THE STRONGMAN?
GET TO IT!

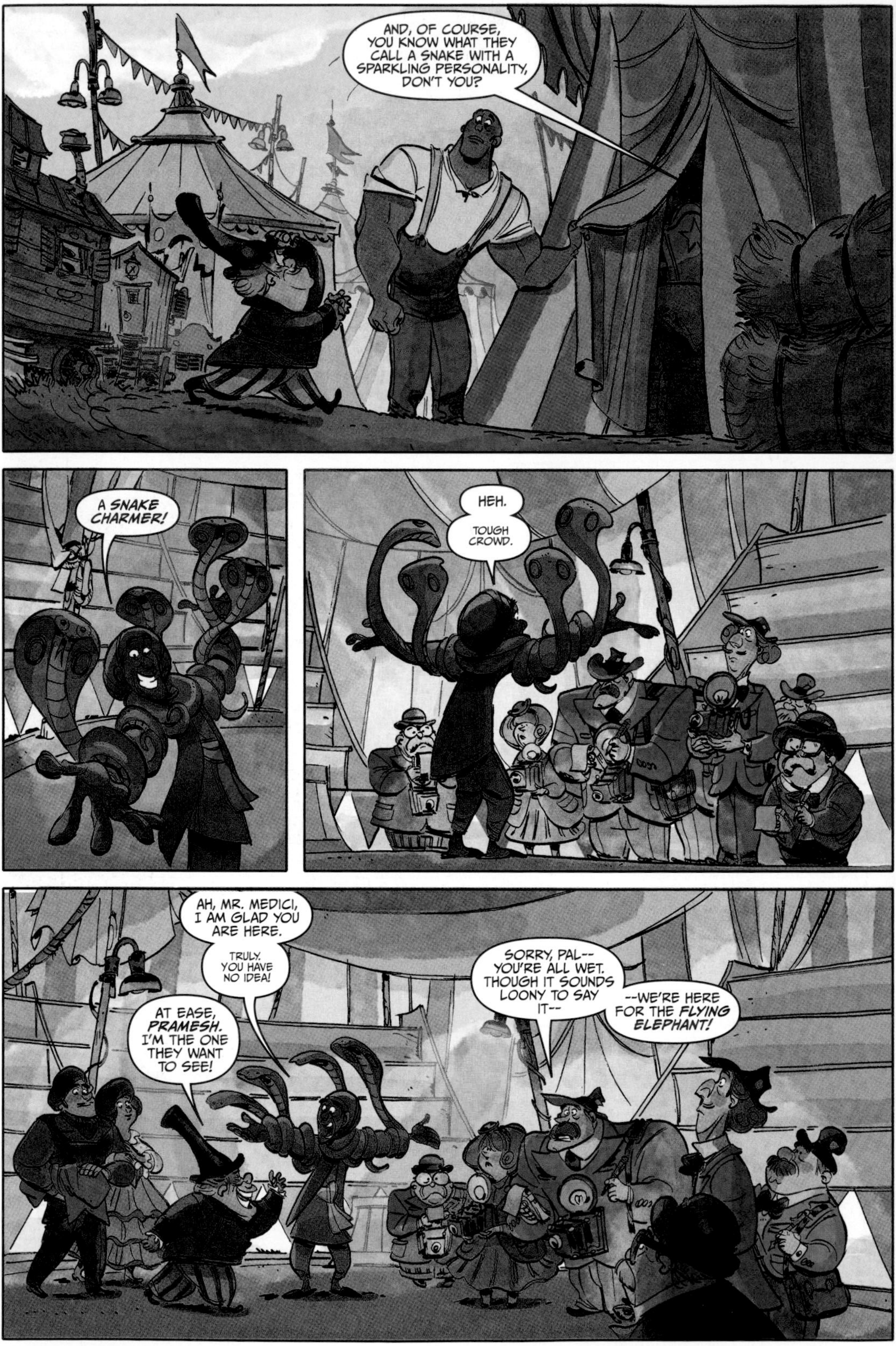
AND, OF COURSE, YOU KNOW WHAT THEY CALL A SNAKE WITH A SPARKLING PERSONALITY, DON'T YOU?
A SNAKE CHARMER!
HEH.
TOUGH CROWD.
AH, MR. MEDICI, I AM GLAD YOU ARE HERE.
TRULY. YOU HAVE NO IDEA!
AT EASE, PRAMESH. I'M THE ONE THEY WANT TO SEE!
SORRY, PAL-- YOU'RE ALL WET. THOUGH IT SOUNDS LOONY TO SAY IT--
--WE'RE HERE FOR THE FLYING ELEPHANT!

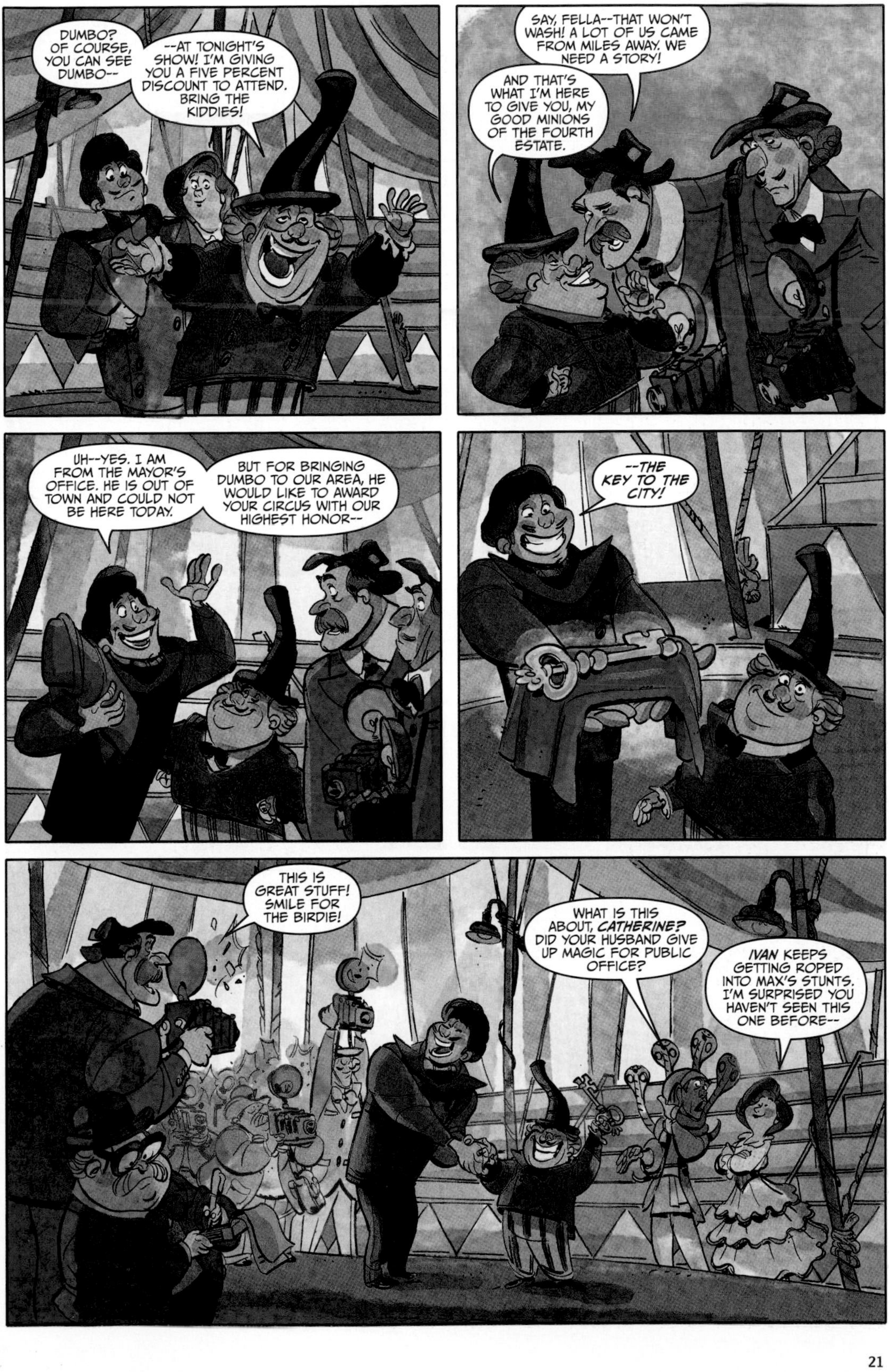
DUMBO? OF COURSE, YOU CAN SEE DUMBO--
--AT TONIGHT'S SHOW! I'M GIVING YOU A FIVE PERCENT DISCOUNT TO ATTEND. BRING THE KIDDIES!
SAY, FELLA--THAT WON'T WASH! A LOT OF US CAME FROM MILES AWAY. WE NEED A STORY!
AND THAT'S WHAT I'M HERE TO GIVE YOU, MY GOOD MINIONS OF THE FOURTH ESTATE.
UH--YES. I AM FROM THE MAYOR'S OFFICE. HE IS OUT OF TOWN AND COULD NOT BE HERE TODAY.
BUT FOR BRINGING DUMBO TO OUR AREA, HE WOULD LIKE TO AWARD YOUR CIRCUS WITH OUR HIGHEST HONOR--
--THE KEY TO THE CITY!
THIS IS GREAT STUFF! SMILE FOR THE BIRDIE!
WHAT IS THIS ABOUT, CATHERINE? DID YOUR HUSBAND GIVE UP MAGIC FOR PUBLIC OFFICE?
IVAN KEEPS GETTING ROPED INTO MAX'S STUNTS. I'M SURPRISED YOU HAVEN'T SEEN THIS ONE BEFORE--

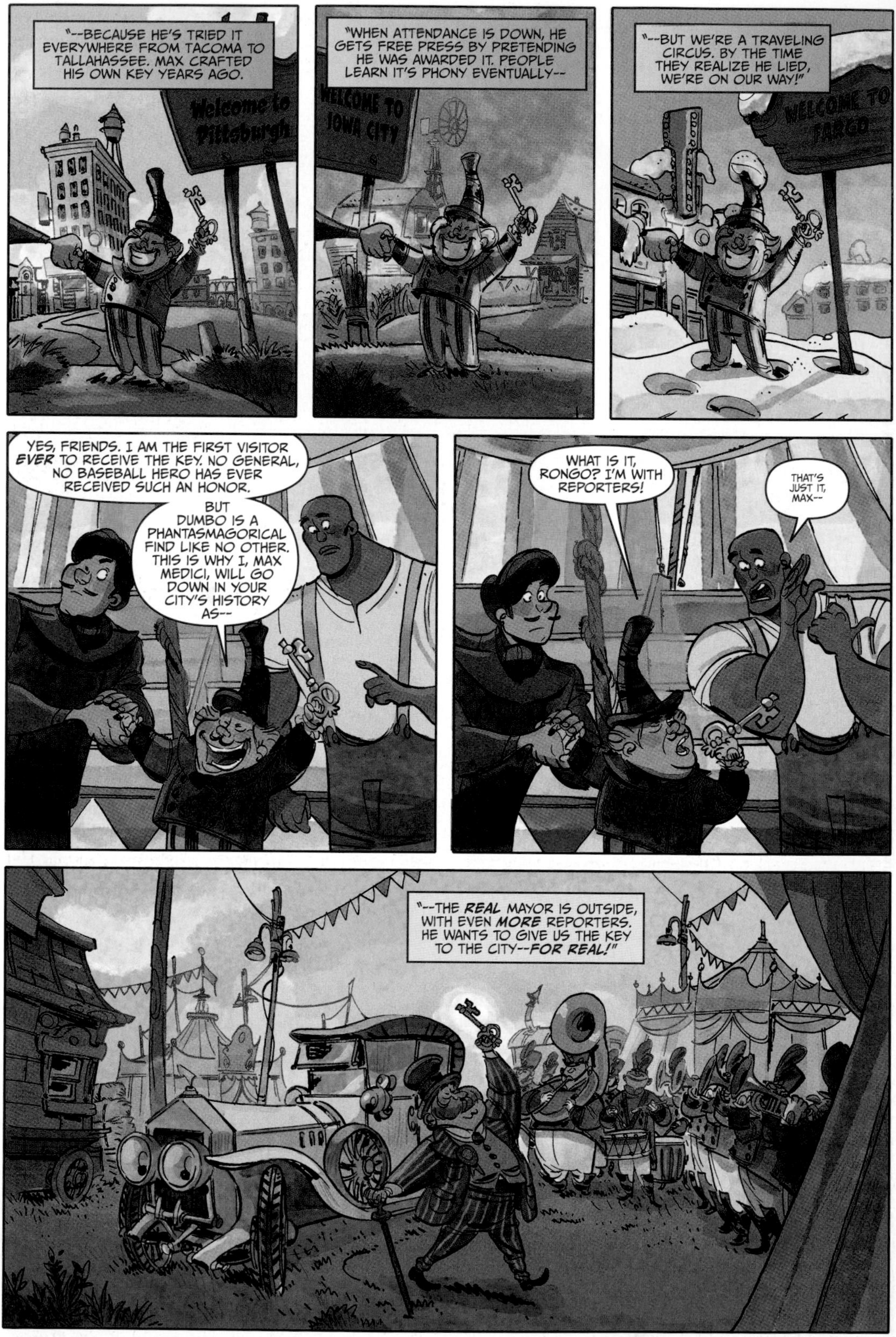
"--BECAUSE HE'S TRIED IT EVERYWHERE FROM TACOMA TO TALLAHASSEE. MAX CRAFTED HIS OWN KEY YEARS AGO.
Welcome to Pittsburgh
"WHEN ATTENDANCE IS DOWN, HE GETS FREE PRESS BY PRETENDING HE WAS AWARDED IT. PEOPLE LEARN IT'S PHONY EVENTUALLY--
WELCOME TO IOWA CITY
"--BUT WE'RE A TRAVELING CIRCUS. BY THE TIME THEY REALIZE HE LIED, WE'RE ON OUR WAY!"
WELCOME TO FARGO
YES, FRIENDS. I AM THE FIRST VISITOR EVER TO RECEIVE THE KEY. NO GENERAL, NO BASEBALL HERO HAS EVER RECEIVED SUCH AN HONOR.
BUT DUMBO IS A PHANTASMAGORICAL FIND LIKE NO OTHER. THIS IS WHY I, MAX MEDICI, WILL GO DOWN IN YOUR CITY'S HISTORY AS--
WHAT IS IT, RONGO? I'M WITH REPORTERS!
THAT'S JUST IT, MAX--
"--THE REAL MAYOR IS OUTSIDE, WITH EVEN MORE REPORTERS. HE WANTS TO GIVE US THE KEY TO THE CITY--FOR REAL!"

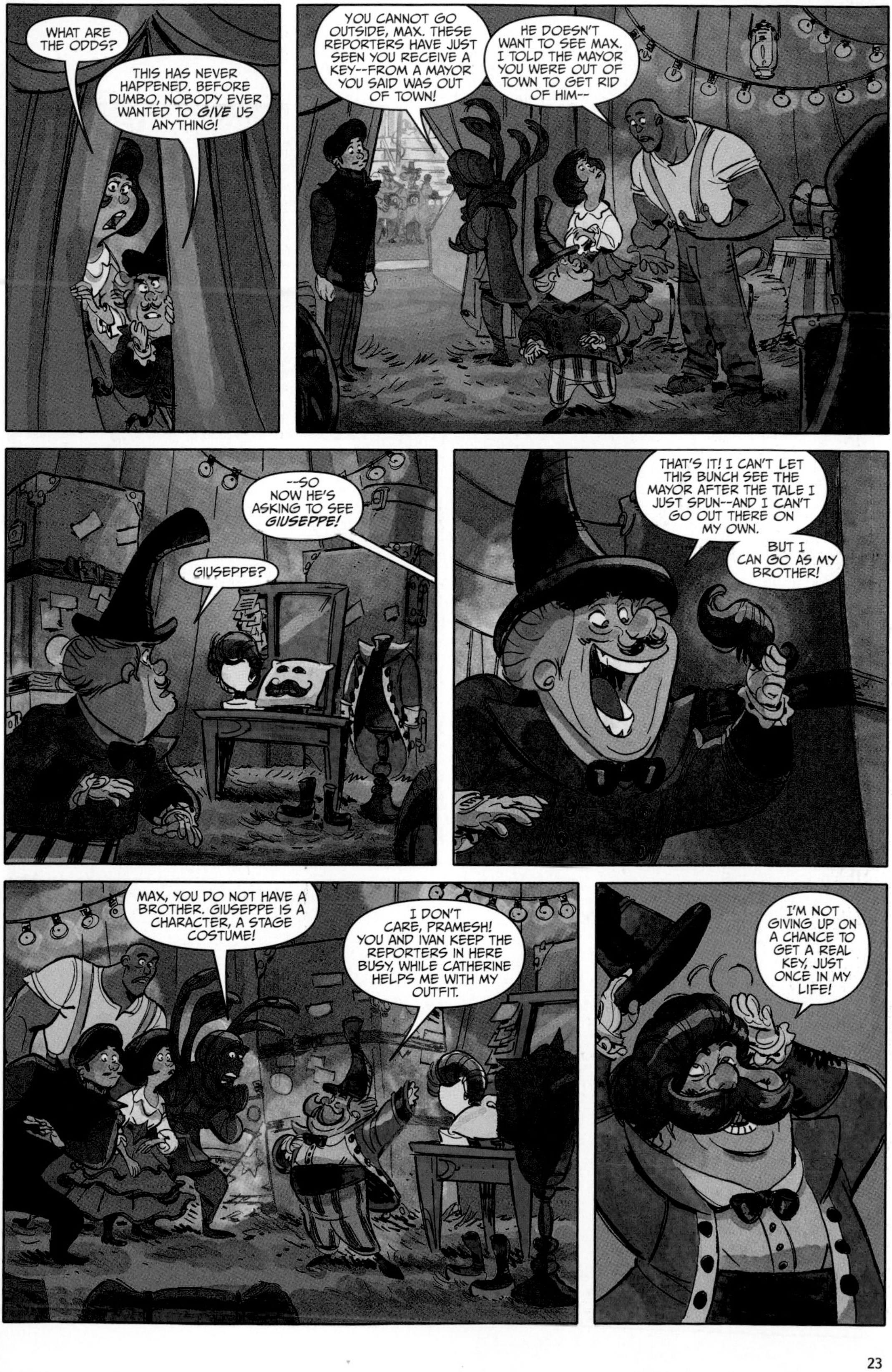
WHAT ARE THE ODDS?
THIS HAS NEVER HAPPENED. BEFORE DUMBO, NOBODY EVER WANTED TO GIVE US ANYTHING!
YOU CANNOT GO OUTSIDE, MAX. THESE REPORTERS HAVE JUST SEEN YOU RECEIVE A KEY--FROM A MAYOR YOU SAID WAS OUT OF TOWN!
HE DOESN'T WANT TO SEE MAX. I TOLD THE MAYOR YOU WERE OUT OF TOWN TO GET RID OF HIM--
--SO NOW HE'S ASKING TO SEE GIUSEPPE!
GIUSEPPE?
THAT'S IT! I CAN'T LET THIS BUNCH SEE THE MAYOR AFTER THE TALE I JUST SPUN--AND I CAN'T GO OUT THERE ON MY OWN.
BUT I CAN GO AS MY BROTHER!
MAX, YOU DO NOT HAVE A BROTHER. GIUSEPPE IS A CHARACTER, A STAGE COSTUME!
I DON'T CARE, PRAMESH! YOU AND IVAN KEEP THE REPORTERS IN HERE BUSY, WHILE CATHERINE HELPS ME WITH MY OUTFIT.
I'M NOT GIVING UP ON A CHANCE TO GET A REAL KEY, JUST ONCE IN MY LIFE!

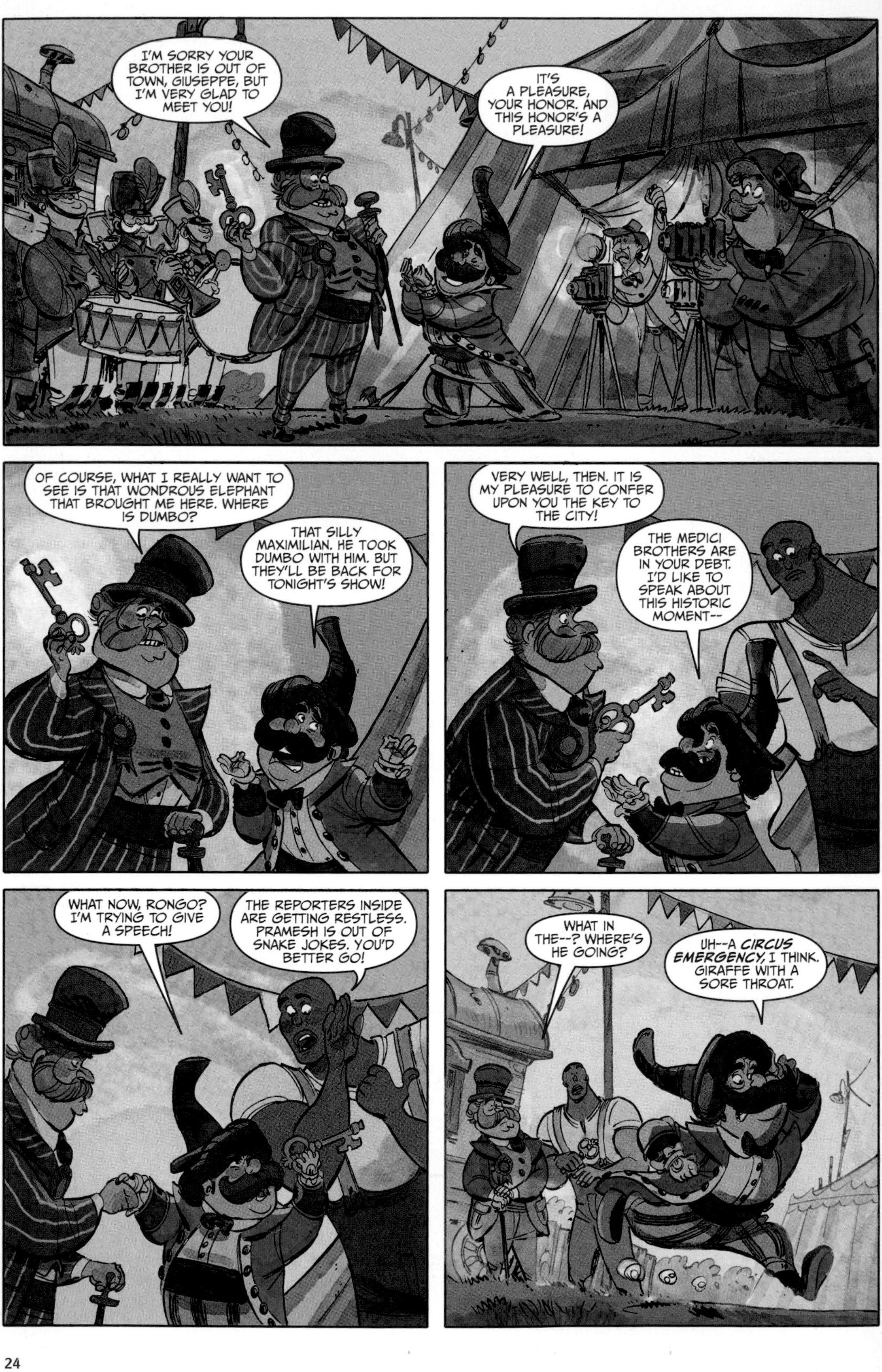
I'M SORRY YOUR BROTHER IS OUT OF TOWN, GIUSEPPE, BUT I'M VERY GLAD TO MEET YOU!
IT'S A PLEASURE, YOUR HONOR. AND THIS HONOR'S A PLEASURE!
OF COURSE, WHAT I REALLY WANT TO SEE IS THAT WONDROUS ELEPHANT THAT BROUGHT ME HERE. WHERE IS DUMBO?
THAT SILLY MAXIMILIAN. HE TOOK DUMBO WITH HIM. BUT THEY'LL BE BACK FOR TONIGHT'S SHOW!
VERY WELL, THEN. IT IS MY PLEASURE TO CONFER UPON YOU THE KEY TO THE CITY!
THE MEDICI BROTHERS ARE IN YOUR DEBT. I'D LIKE TO SPEAK ABOUT THIS HISTORIC MOMENT--
WHAT NOW, RONGO? I'M TRYING TO GIVE A SPEECH!
THE REPORTERS INSIDE ARE GETTING RESTLESS. PRAMESH IS OUT OF SNAKE JOKES. YOU'D BETTER GO!
WHAT IN THE--? WHERE'S HE GOING?
UH--A *CIRCUS EMERGENCY,* I THINK. GIRAFFE WITH A SORE THROAT.

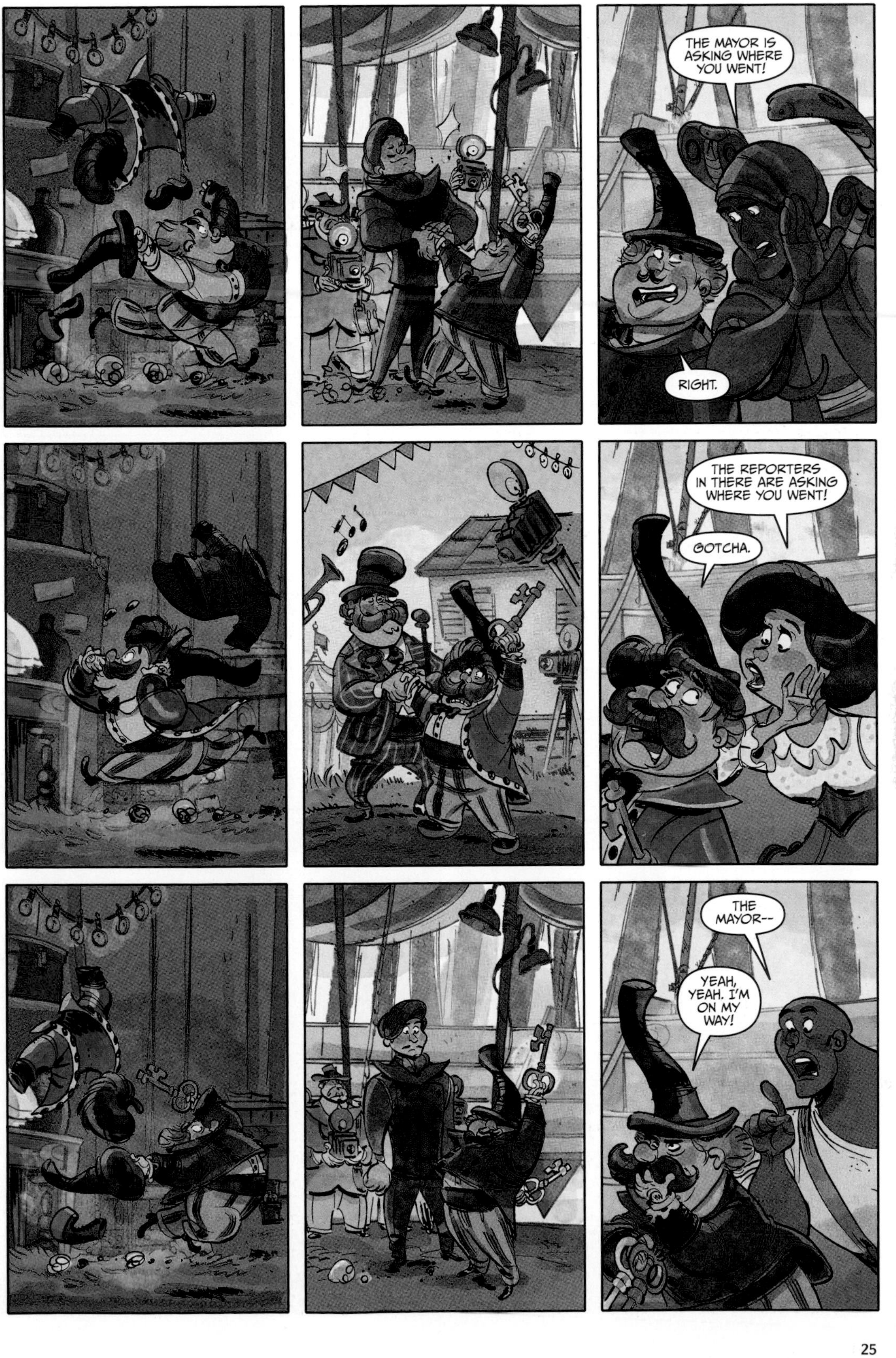
THE MAYOR IS ASKING WHERE YOU WENT!
RIGHT.
THE REPORTERS IN THERE ARE ASKING WHERE YOU WENT!
GOTCHA.
THE MAYOR--
YEAH, YEAH. I'M ON MY WAY!

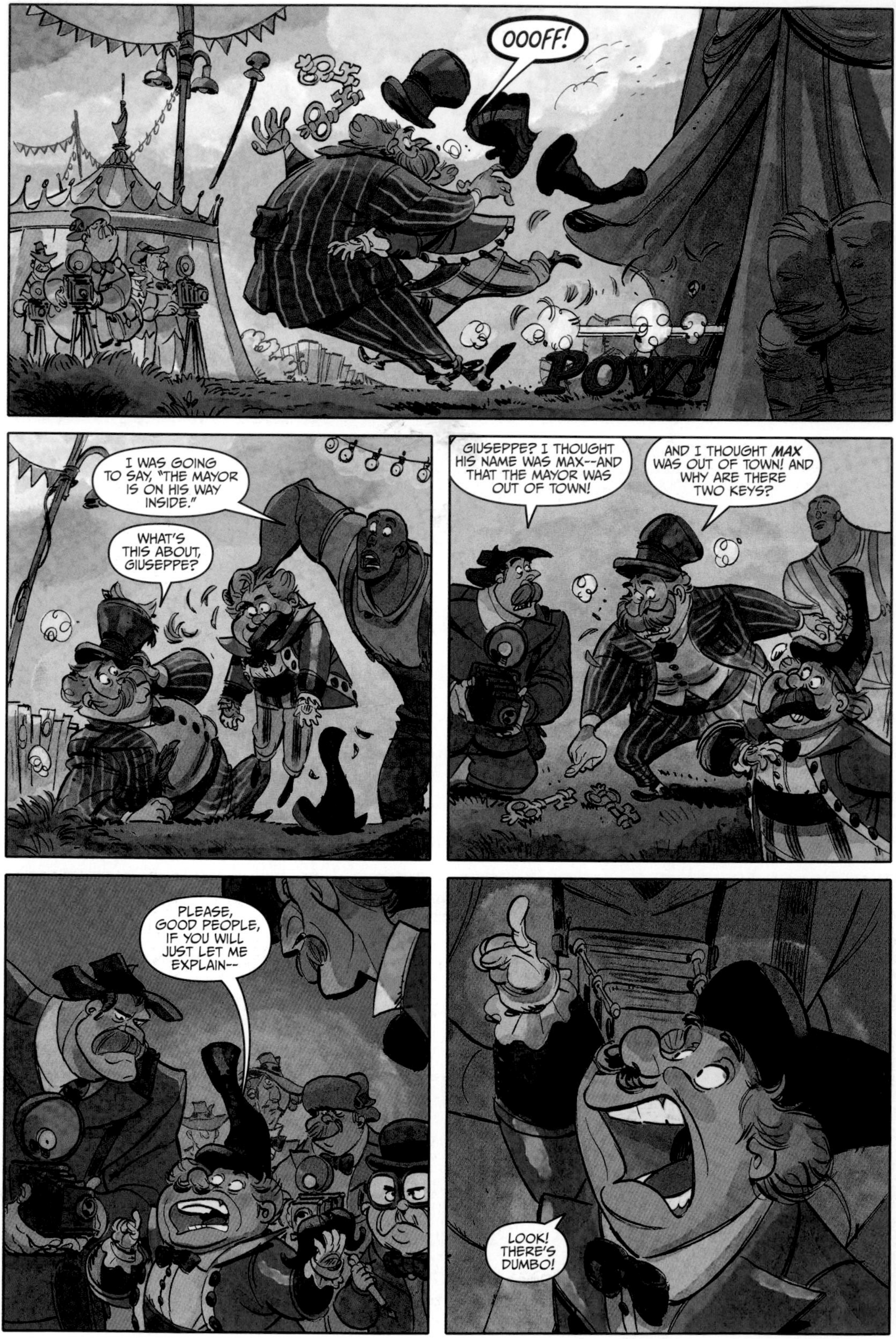
OOOFF!
POW!
I WAS GOING TO SAY, "THE MAYOR IS ON HIS WAY INSIDE."
WHAT'S THIS ABOUT, GIUSEPPE?
GIUSEPPE? I THOUGHT HIS NAME WAS MAX--AND THAT THE MAYOR WAS OUT OF TOWN!
AND I THOUGHT MAX WAS OUT OF TOWN! AND WHY ARE THERE TWO KEYS?
PLEASE, GOOD PEOPLE, IF YOU WILL JUST LET ME EXPLAIN--
LOOK! THERE'S DUMBO!

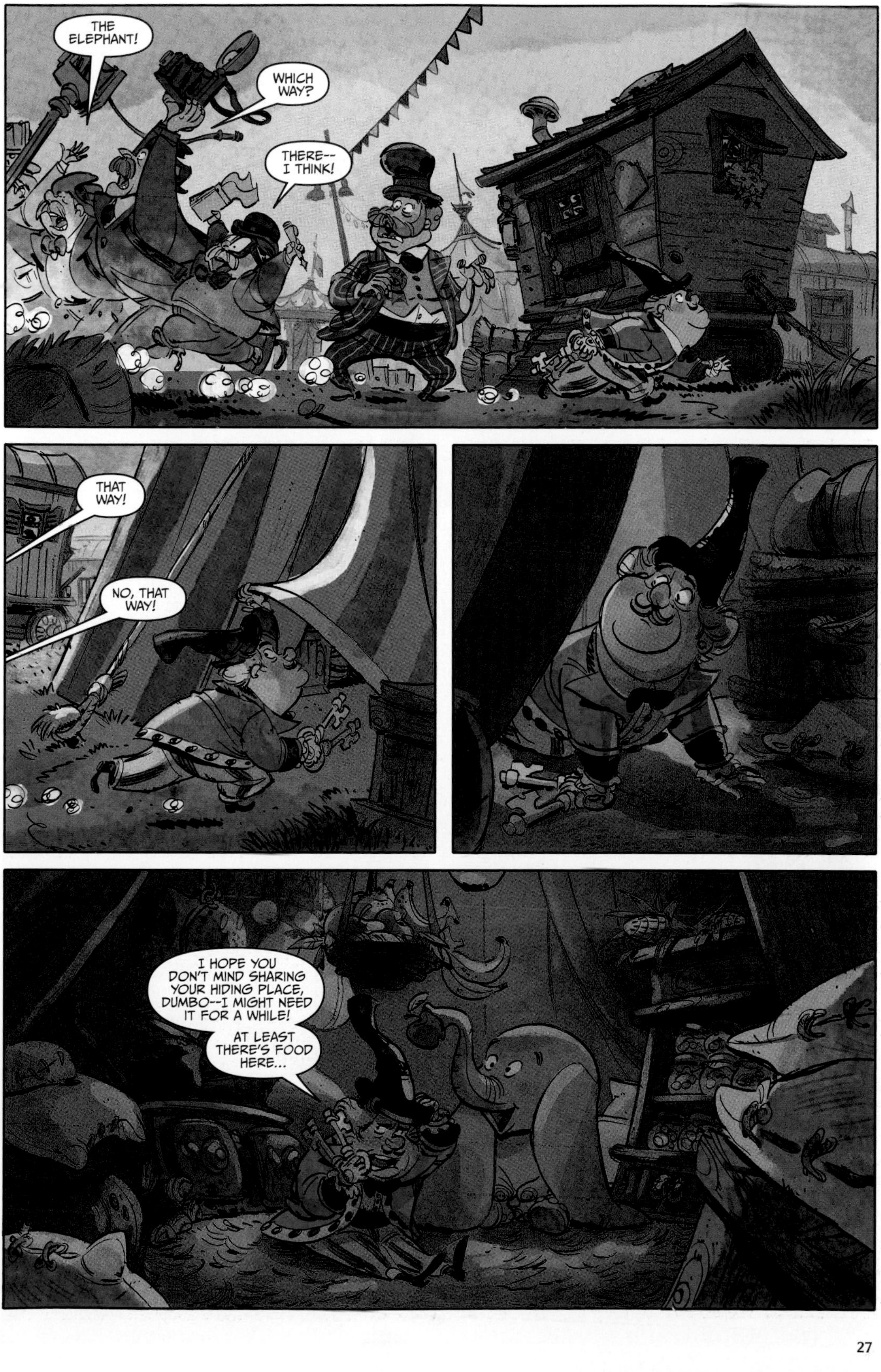
THE ELEPHANT!
WHICH WAY?
THERE-- I THINK!
THAT WAY!
NO, THAT WAY!
I HOPE YOU DON'T MIND SHARING YOUR HIDING PLACE, DUMBO--I MIGHT NEED IT FOR A WHILE!
AT LEAST THERE'S FOOD HERE...

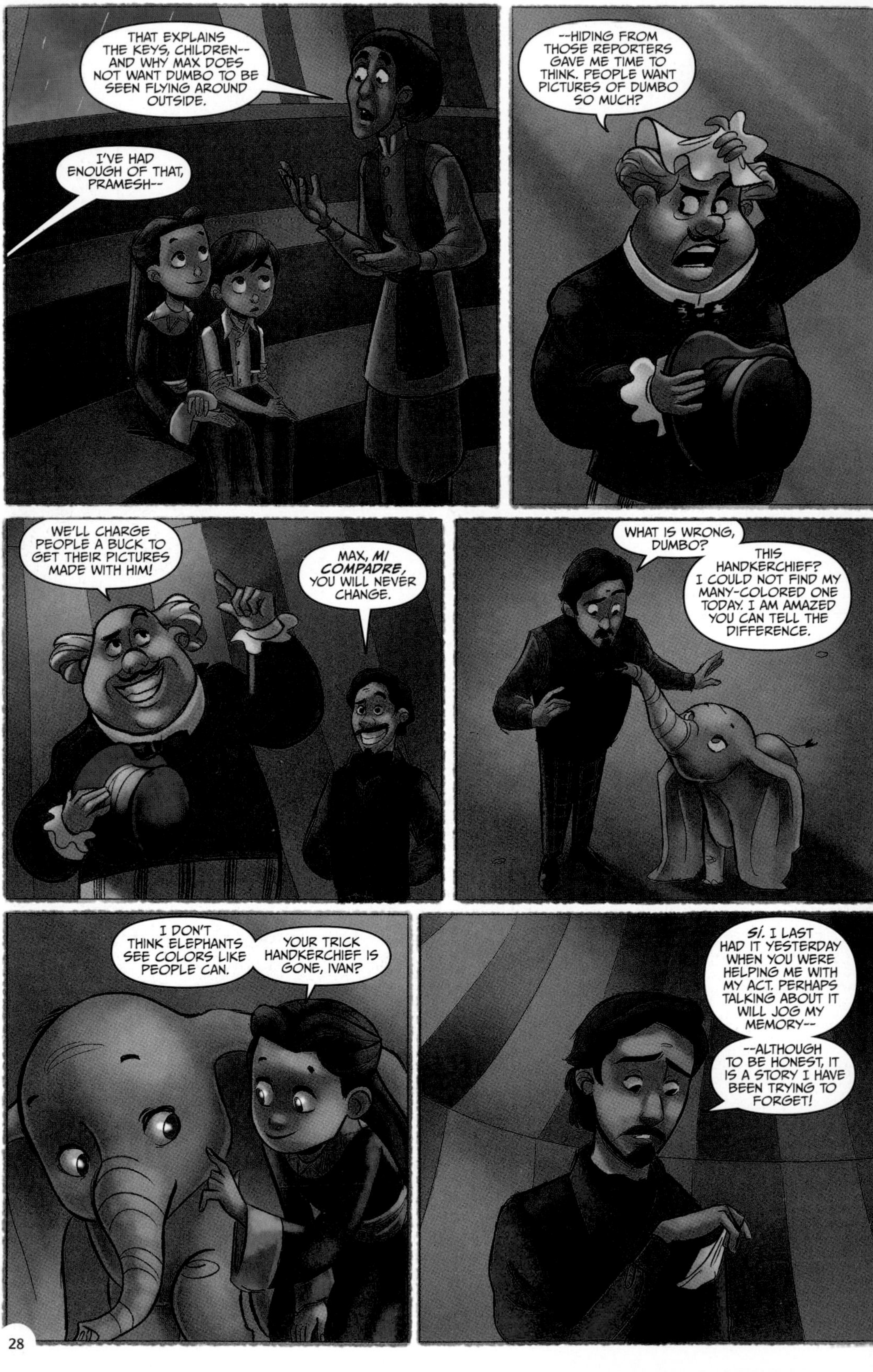
THAT EXPLAINS THE KEYS, CHILDREN-- AND WHY MAX DOES NOT WANT DUMBO TO BE SEEN FLYING AROUND OUTSIDE.
I'VE HAD ENOUGH OF THAT, PRAMESH--
--HIDING FROM THOSE REPORTERS GAVE ME TIME TO THINK. PEOPLE WANT PICTURES OF DUMBO SO MUCH?
WE'LL CHARGE PEOPLE A BUCK TO GET THEIR PICTURES MADE WITH HIM!
MAX, *MI COMPADRE*, YOU WILL NEVER CHANGE.
WHAT IS WRONG, DUMBO?
THIS HANDKERCHIEF? I COULD NOT FIND MY MANY-COLORED ONE TODAY. I AM AMAZED YOU CAN TELL THE DIFFERENCE.
I DON'T THINK ELEPHANTS SEE COLORS LIKE PEOPLE CAN.
YOUR TRICK HANDKERCHIEF IS GONE, IVAN?
SÍ. I LAST HAD IT YESTERDAY WHEN YOU WERE HELPING ME WITH MY ACT. PERHAPS TALKING ABOUT IT WILL JOG MY MEMORY--
--ALTHOUGH TO BE HONEST, IT IS A STORY I HAVE BEEN TRYING TO FORGET!

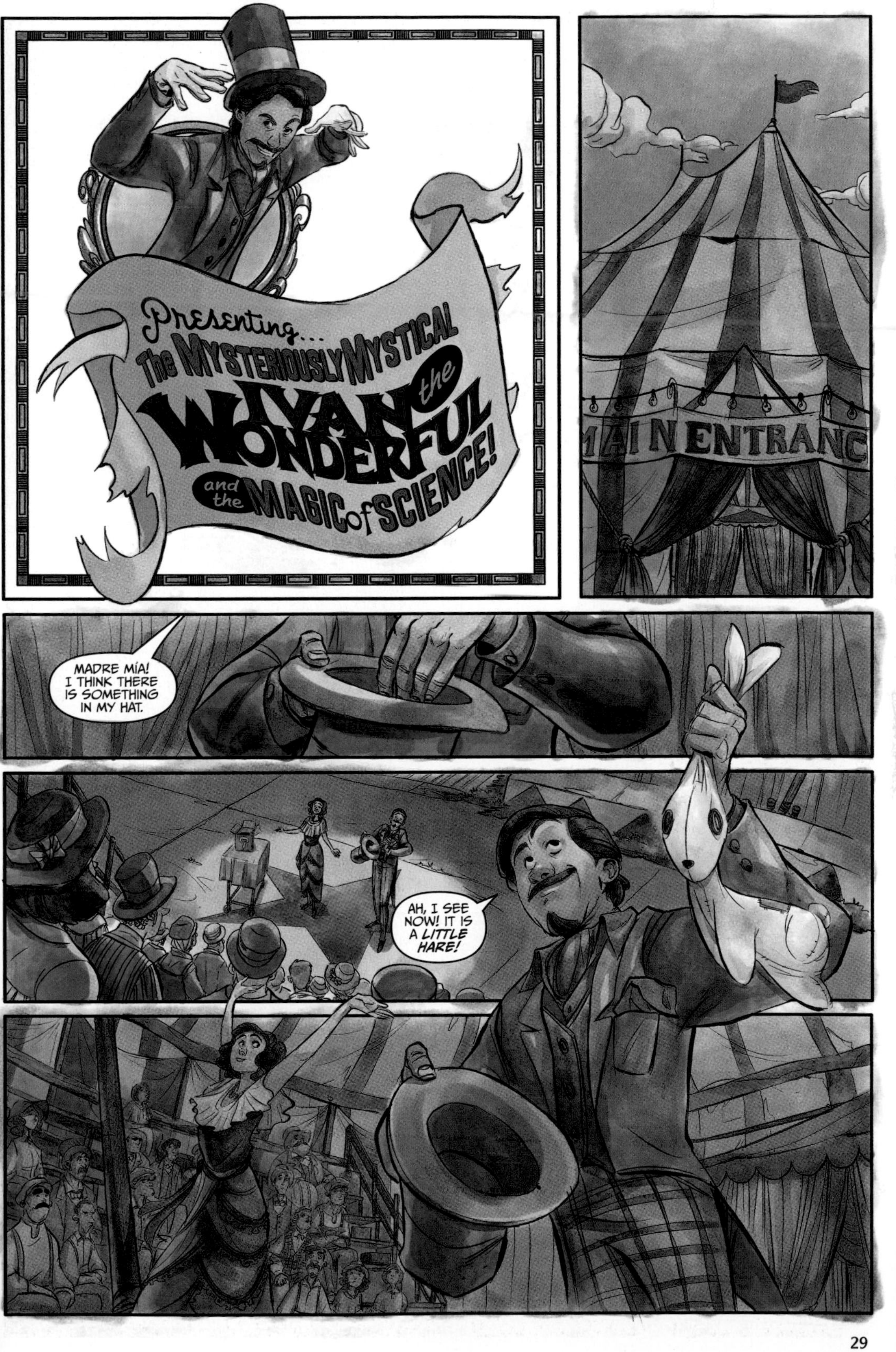
Presenting... The Mysteriously Mystical Ivan the Wonderful and the Magic of Science!
MAIN ENTRANC
MADRE MÍA! I THINK THERE IS SOMETHING IN MY HAT.
AH, I SEE NOW! IT IS A *LITTLE HARE!*

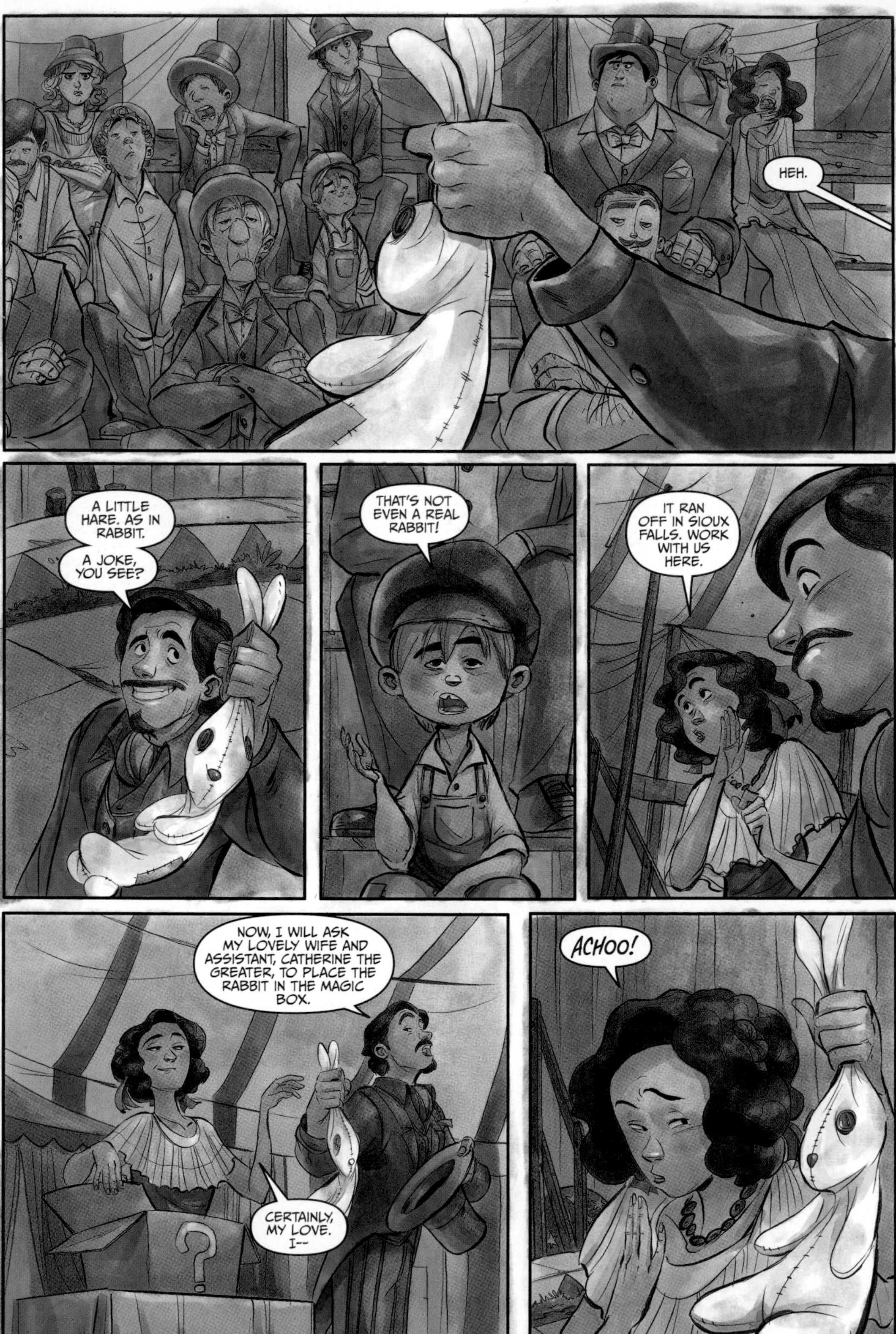

HEH.
A LITTLE HARE. AS IN RABBIT.
A JOKE, YOU SEE?
THAT'S NOT EVEN A REAL RABBIT!
IT RAN OFF IN SIOUX FALLS. WORK WITH US HERE.
NOW, I WILL ASK MY LOVELY WIFE AND ASSISTANT, CATHERINE THE GREATER, TO PLACE THE RABBIT IN THE MAGIC BOX.
CERTAINLY, MY LOVE. I--
ACHOO!

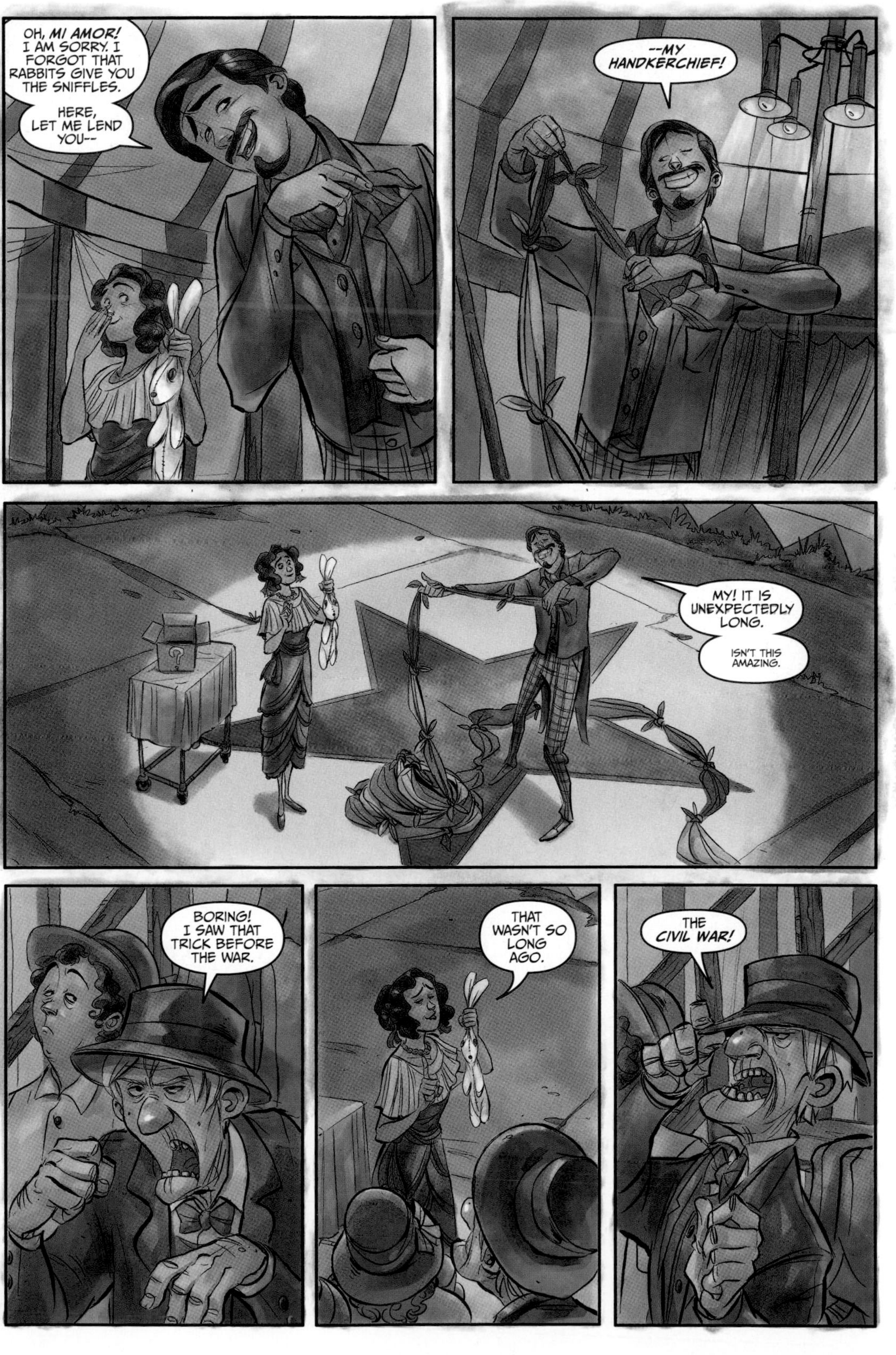
OH, *MI AMOR!* I AM SORRY. I FORGOT THAT RABBITS GIVE YOU THE SNIFFLES.
HERE, LET ME LEND YOU--
--MY *HANDKERCHIEF!*
MY! IT IS UNEXPECTEDLY LONG.
ISN'T THIS AMAZING.
BORING! I SAW THAT TRICK BEFORE THE WAR.
THAT WASN'T SO LONG AGO.
THE *CIVIL WAR!*

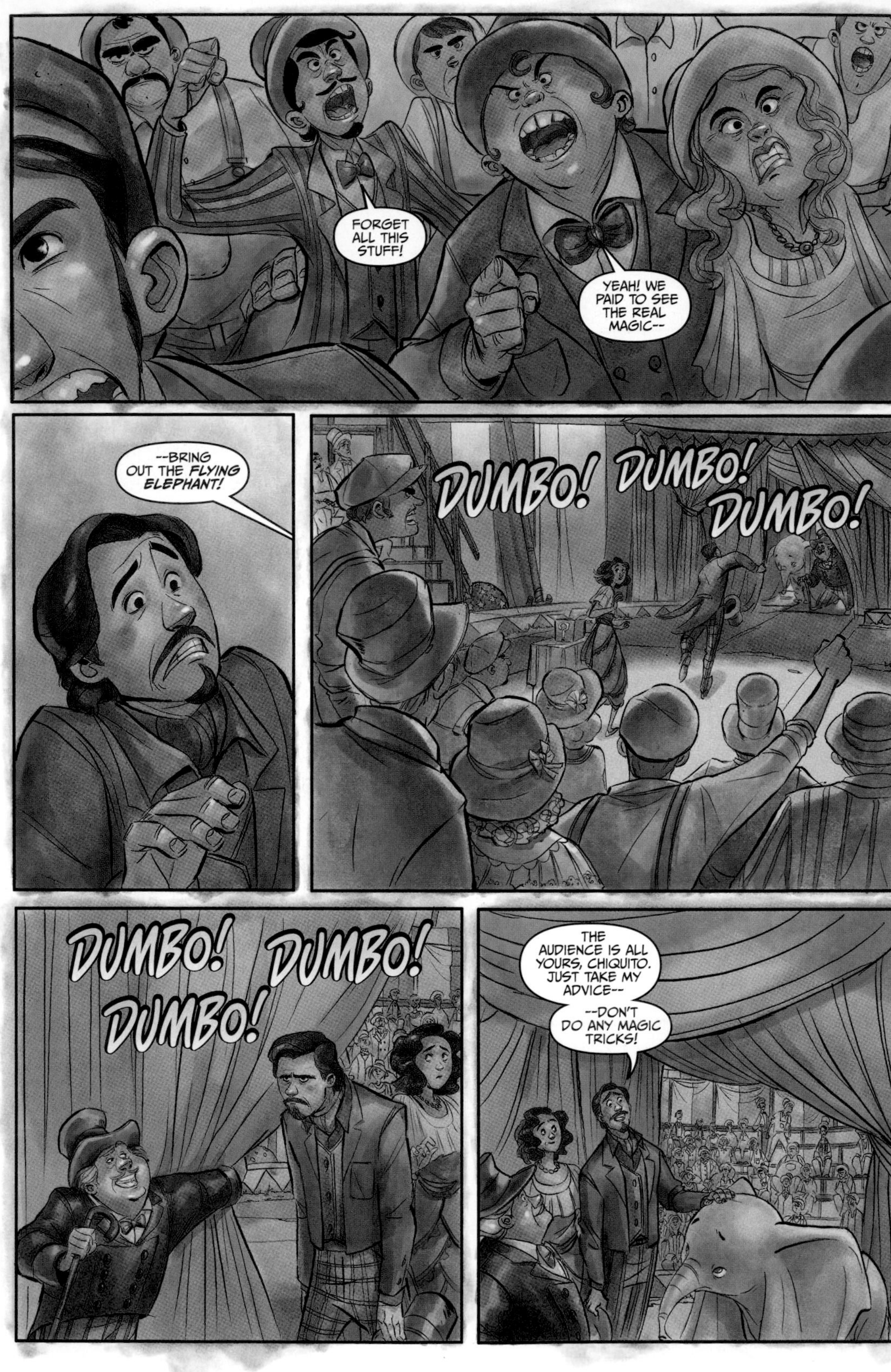
FORGET ALL THIS STUFF!
YEAH! WE PAID TO SEE THE REAL MAGIC--
--BRING OUT THE *FLYING ELEPHANT!*
DUMBO! DUMBO! DUMBO!
DUMBO! DUMBO! DUMBO!
THE AUDIENCE IS ALL YOURS, CHIQUITO. JUST TAKE MY ADVICE--
--DON'T DO ANY MAGIC TRICKS!

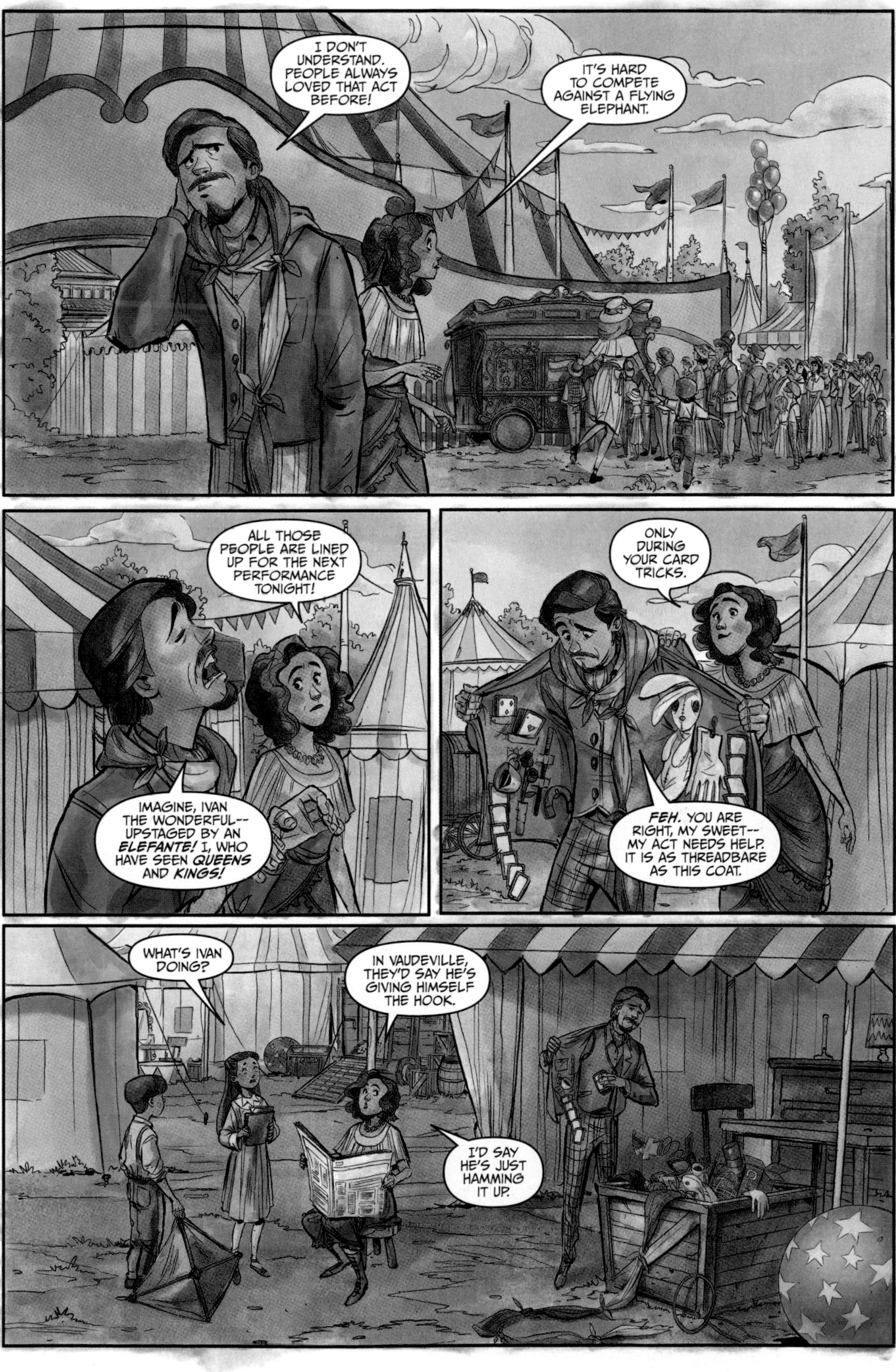

I DON'T UNDERSTAND. PEOPLE ALWAYS LOVED THAT ACT BEFORE!
IT'S HARD TO COMPETE AGAINST A FLYING ELEPHANT.
ALL THOSE PEOPLE ARE LINED UP FOR THE NEXT PERFORMANCE TONIGHT!
IMAGINE, IVAN THE WONDERFUL--UPSTAGED BY AN *ELEFANTE!* I, WHO HAVE SEEN *QUEENS* AND *KINGS!*
ONLY DURING YOUR CARD TRICKS.
FEH. YOU ARE RIGHT, MY SWEET--MY ACT NEEDS HELP. IT IS AS THREADBARE AS THIS COAT.
WHAT'S IVAN DOING?
IN VAUDEVILLE, THEY'D SAY HE'S GIVING HIMSELF THE HOOK.
I'D SAY HE'S JUST HAMMING IT UP.

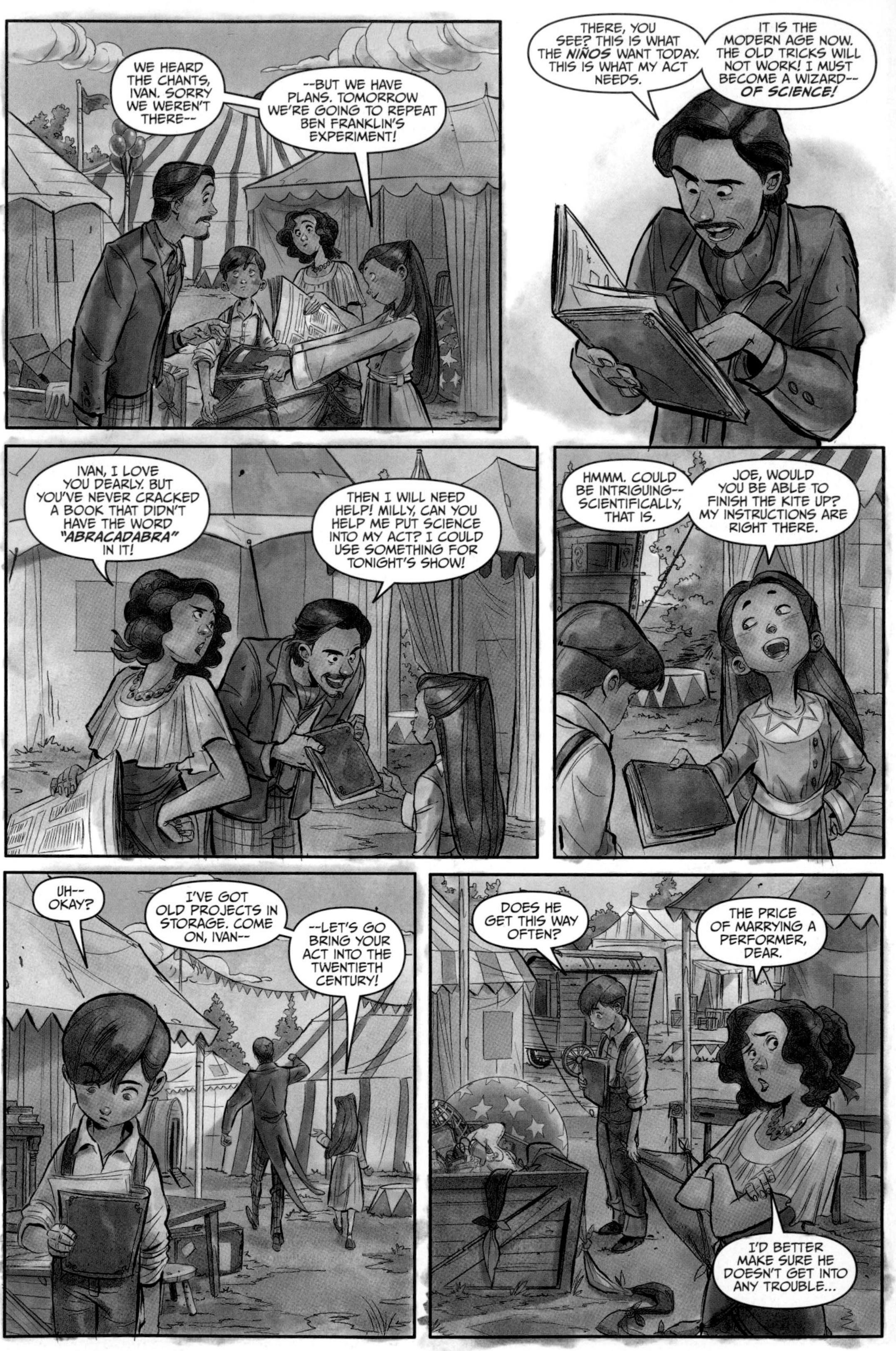
WE HEARD THE CHANTS, IVAN. SORRY WE WEREN'T THERE--
--BUT WE HAVE PLANS. TOMORROW WE'RE GOING TO REPEAT BEN FRANKLIN'S EXPERIMENT!
THERE, YOU SEE? THIS IS WHAT THE *NIÑOS* WANT TODAY. THIS IS WHAT MY ACT NEEDS.
IT IS THE MODERN AGE NOW. THE OLD TRICKS WILL NOT WORK! I MUST BECOME A WIZARD-- ***OF SCIENCE!***
IVAN, I LOVE YOU DEARLY. BUT YOU'VE NEVER CRACKED A BOOK THAT DIDN'T HAVE THE WORD ***"ABRACADABRA"*** IN IT!
THEN I WILL NEED HELP! MILLY, CAN YOU HELP ME PUT SCIENCE INTO MY ACT? I COULD USE SOMETHING FOR TONIGHT'S SHOW!
HMMM. COULD BE INTRIGUING-- SCIENTIFICALLY, THAT IS.
JOE, WOULD YOU BE ABLE TO FINISH THE KITE UP? MY INSTRUCTIONS ARE RIGHT THERE.
UH-- OKAY?
I'VE GOT OLD PROJECTS IN STORAGE. COME ON, IVAN--
--LET'S GO BRING YOUR ACT INTO THE TWENTIETH CENTURY!
DOES HE GET THIS WAY OFTEN?
THE PRICE OF MARRYING A PERFORMER, DEAR.
I'D BETTER MAKE SURE HE DOESN'T GET INTO ANY TROUBLE...

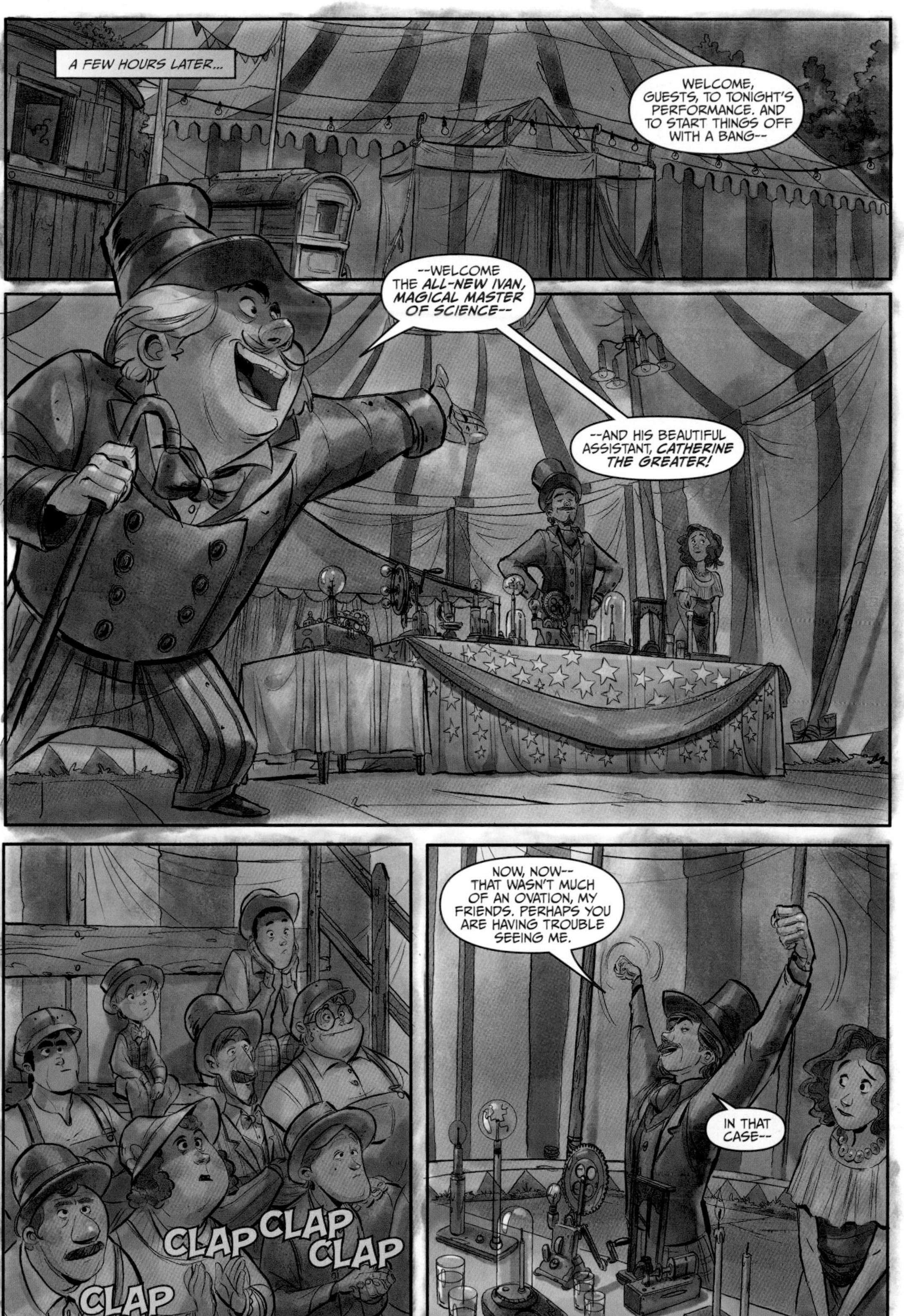
A FEW HOURS LATER...
WELCOME, GUESTS, TO TONIGHT'S PERFORMANCE. AND TO START THINGS OFF WITH A BANG--
--WELCOME THE ALL-NEW IVAN, MAGICAL MASTER OF SCIENCE--
--AND HIS BEAUTIFUL ASSISTANT, CATHERINE THE GREATER!
CLAP CLAP
CLAP
CLAP
NOW, NOW-- THAT WASN'T MUCH OF AN OVATION, MY FRIENDS. PERHAPS YOU ARE HAVING TROUBLE SEEING ME.
IN THAT CASE--

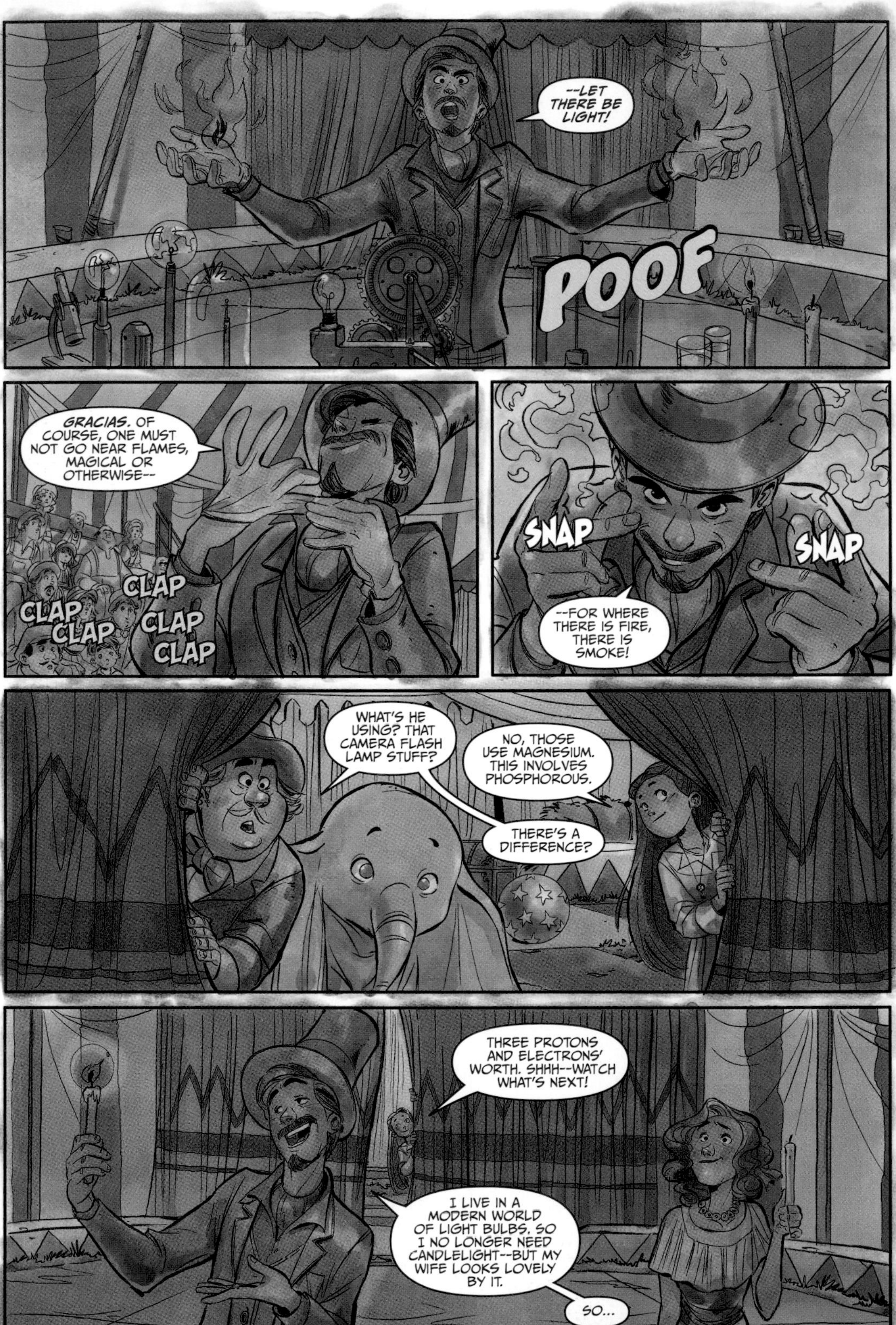
--LET THERE BE LIGHT!
POOF
GRACIAS. OF COURSE, ONE MUST NOT GO NEAR FLAMES, MAGICAL OR OTHERWISE--
CLAP CLAP CLAP CLAP CLAP
SNAP SNAP
--FOR WHERE THERE IS FIRE, THERE IS SMOKE!
WHAT'S HE USING? THAT CAMERA FLASH LAMP STUFF?
NO, THOSE USE MAGNESIUM. THIS INVOLVES PHOSPHOROUS.
THERE'S A DIFFERENCE?
THREE PROTONS AND ELECTRONS' WORTH. SHHH--WATCH WHAT'S NEXT!
I LIVE IN A MODERN WORLD OF LIGHT BULBS. SO I NO LONGER NEED CANDLELIGHT--BUT MY WIFE LOOKS LOVELY BY IT.
SO...

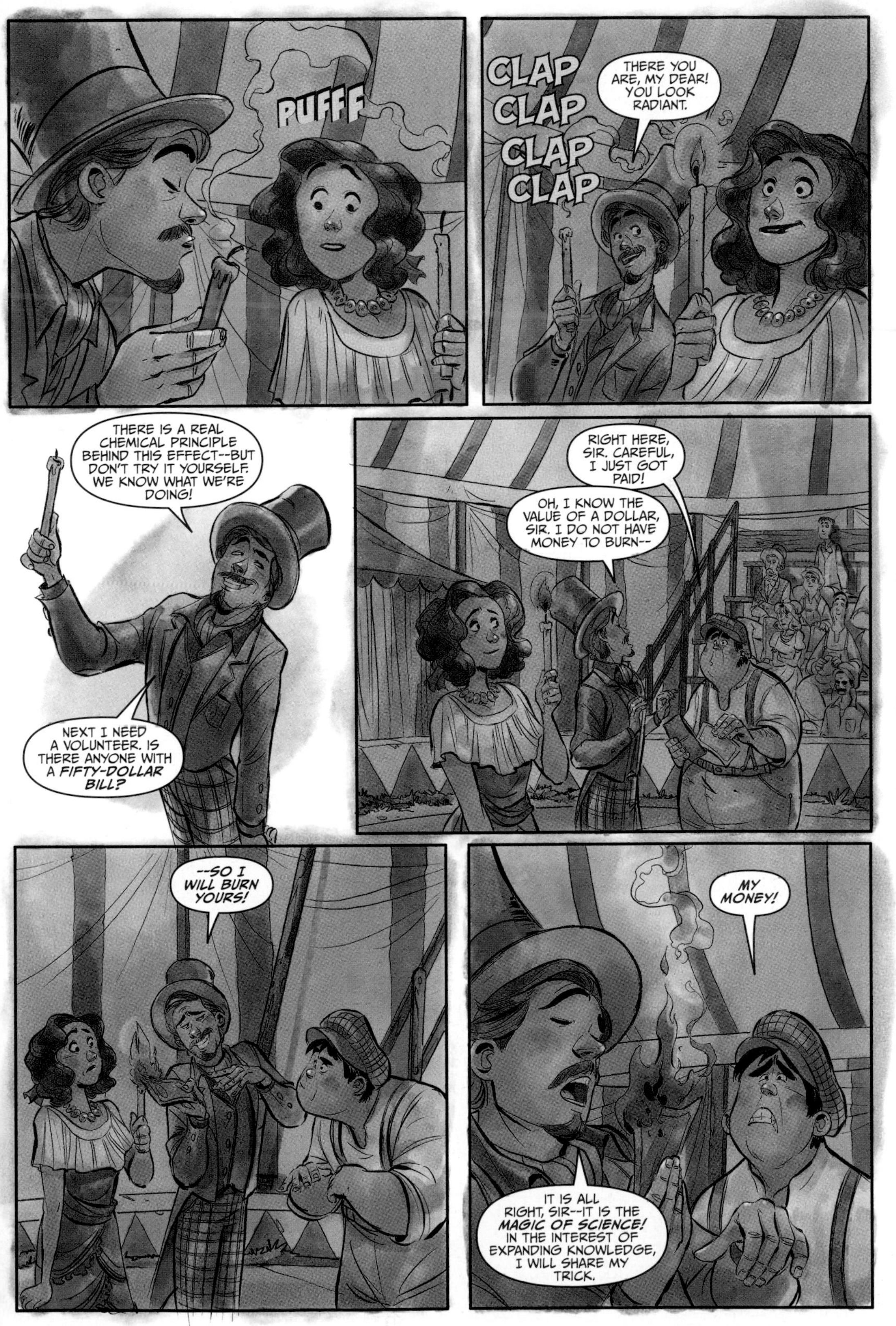
PUFFF
CLAP
CLAP
CLAP
CLAP
THERE YOU ARE, MY DEAR! YOU LOOK RADIANT.
THERE IS A REAL CHEMICAL PRINCIPLE BEHIND THIS EFFECT--BUT DON'T TRY IT YOURSELF. WE KNOW WHAT WE'RE DOING!
NEXT I NEED A VOLUNTEER. IS THERE ANYONE WITH A FIFTY-DOLLAR BILL?
RIGHT HERE, SIR. CAREFUL, I JUST GOT PAID!
OH, I KNOW THE VALUE OF A DOLLAR, SIR. I DO NOT HAVE MONEY TO BURN--
--SO I WILL BURN YOURS!
MY MONEY!
IT IS ALL RIGHT, SIR--IT IS THE MAGIC OF SCIENCE! IN THE INTEREST OF EXPANDING KNOWLEDGE, I WILL SHARE MY TRICK.

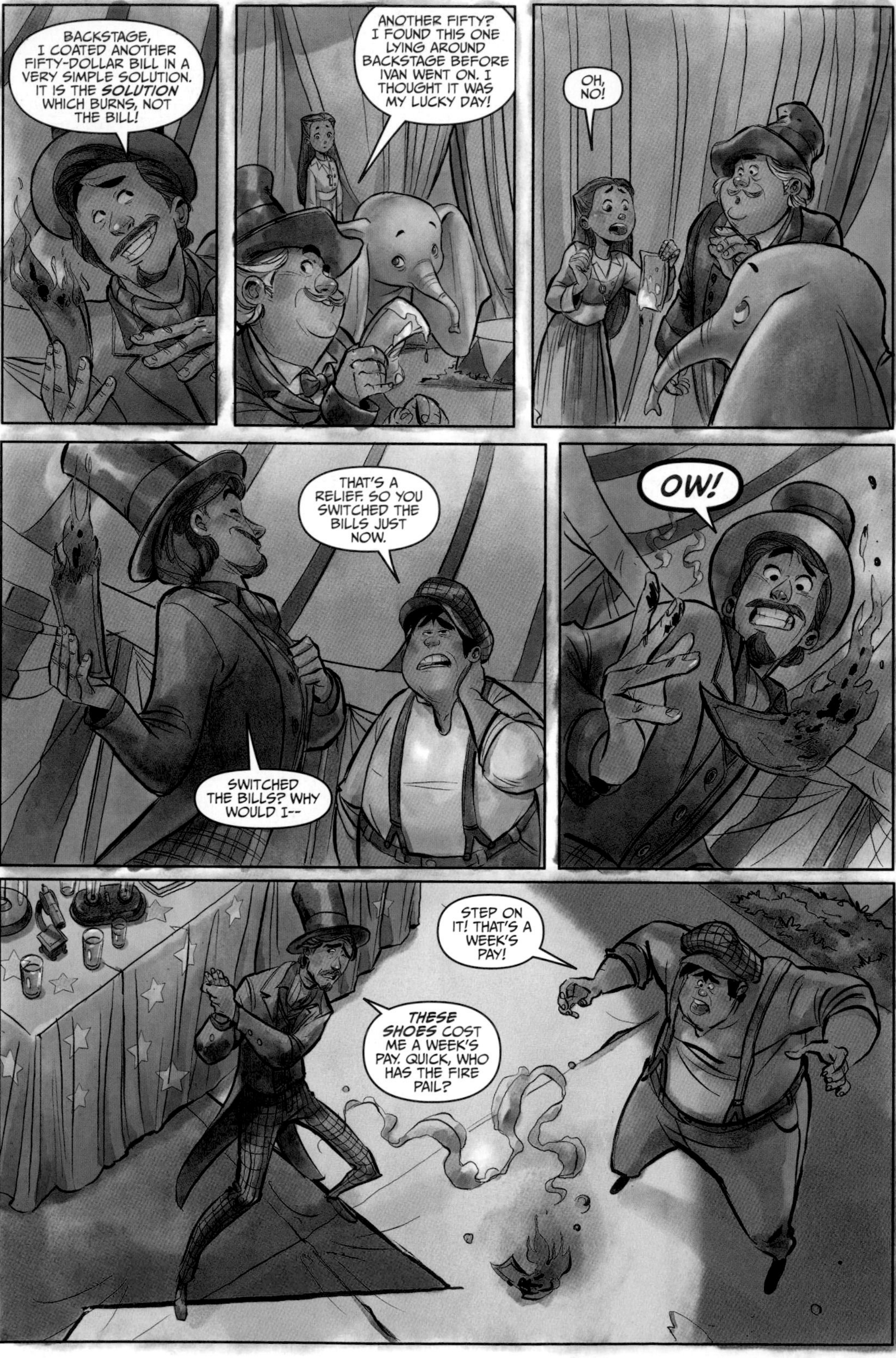
BACKSTAGE, I COATED ANOTHER FIFTY-DOLLAR BILL IN A VERY SIMPLE SOLUTION. IT IS THE *SOLUTION* WHICH BURNS, NOT THE BILL!
ANOTHER FIFTY? I FOUND THIS ONE LYING AROUND BACKSTAGE BEFORE IVAN WENT ON. I THOUGHT IT WAS MY LUCKY DAY!
OH, NO!
THAT'S A RELIEF. SO YOU SWITCHED THE BILLS JUST NOW.
SWITCHED THE BILLS? WHY WOULD I--
OW!
STEP ON IT! THAT'S A WEEK'S PAY!
THESE SHOES COST ME A WEEK'S PAY. QUICK, WHO HAS THE FIRE PAIL?

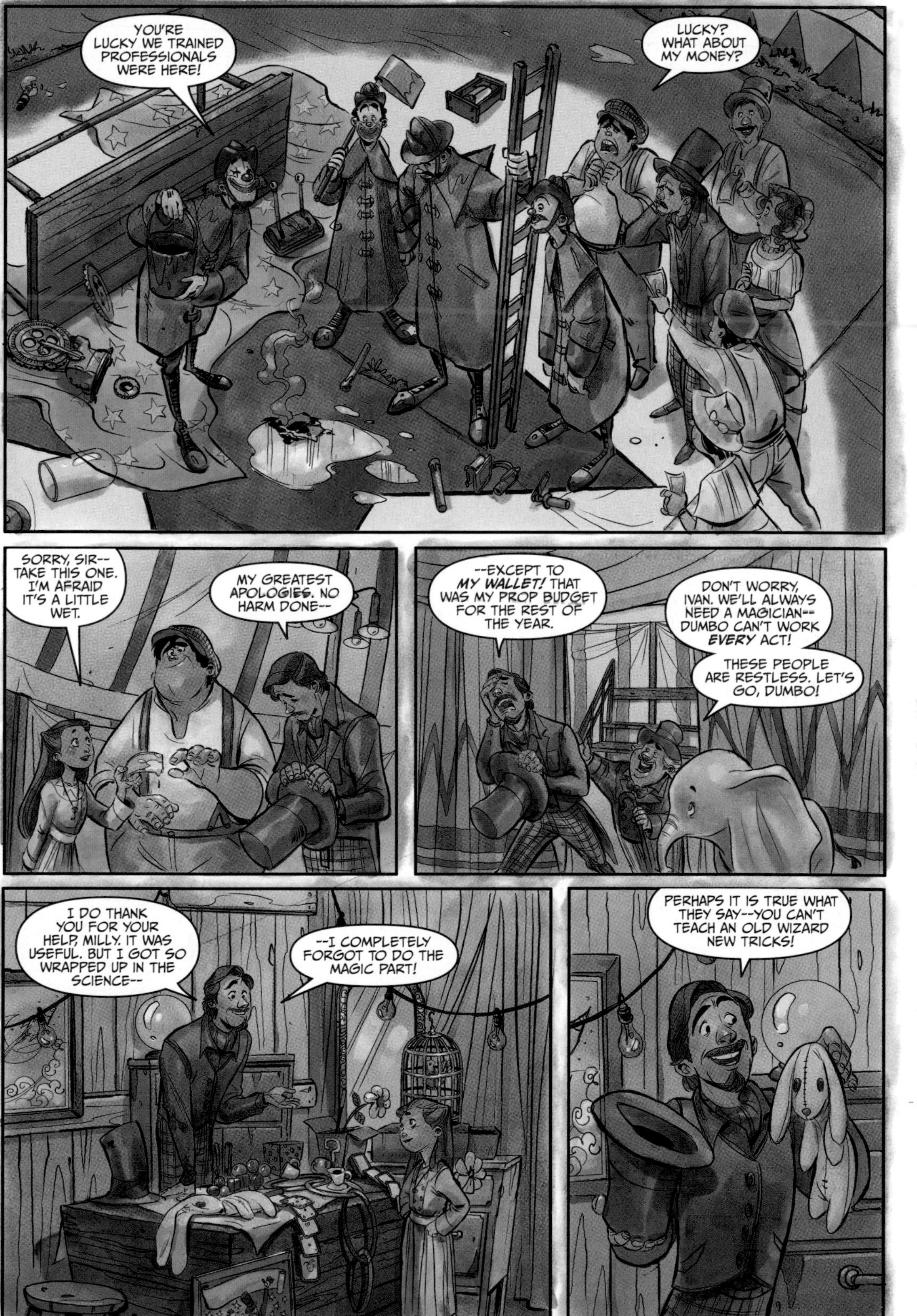
YOU'RE LUCKY WE TRAINED PROFESSIONALS WERE HERE!
LUCKY? WHAT ABOUT MY MONEY?
SORRY, SIR-- TAKE THIS ONE. I'M AFRAID IT'S A LITTLE WET.
MY GREATEST APOLOGIES. NO HARM DONE--
--EXCEPT TO MY WALLET! THAT WAS MY PROP BUDGET FOR THE REST OF THE YEAR.
DON'T WORRY, IVAN. WE'LL ALWAYS NEED A MAGICIAN-- DUMBO CAN'T WORK EVERY ACT!
THESE PEOPLE ARE RESTLESS. LET'S GO, DUMBO!
I DO THANK YOU FOR YOUR HELP, MILLY. IT WAS USEFUL. BUT I GOT SO WRAPPED UP IN THE SCIENCE--
--I COMPLETELY FORGOT TO DO THE MAGIC PART!
PERHAPS IT IS TRUE WHAT THEY SAY--YOU CAN'T TEACH AN OLD WIZARD NEW TRICKS!

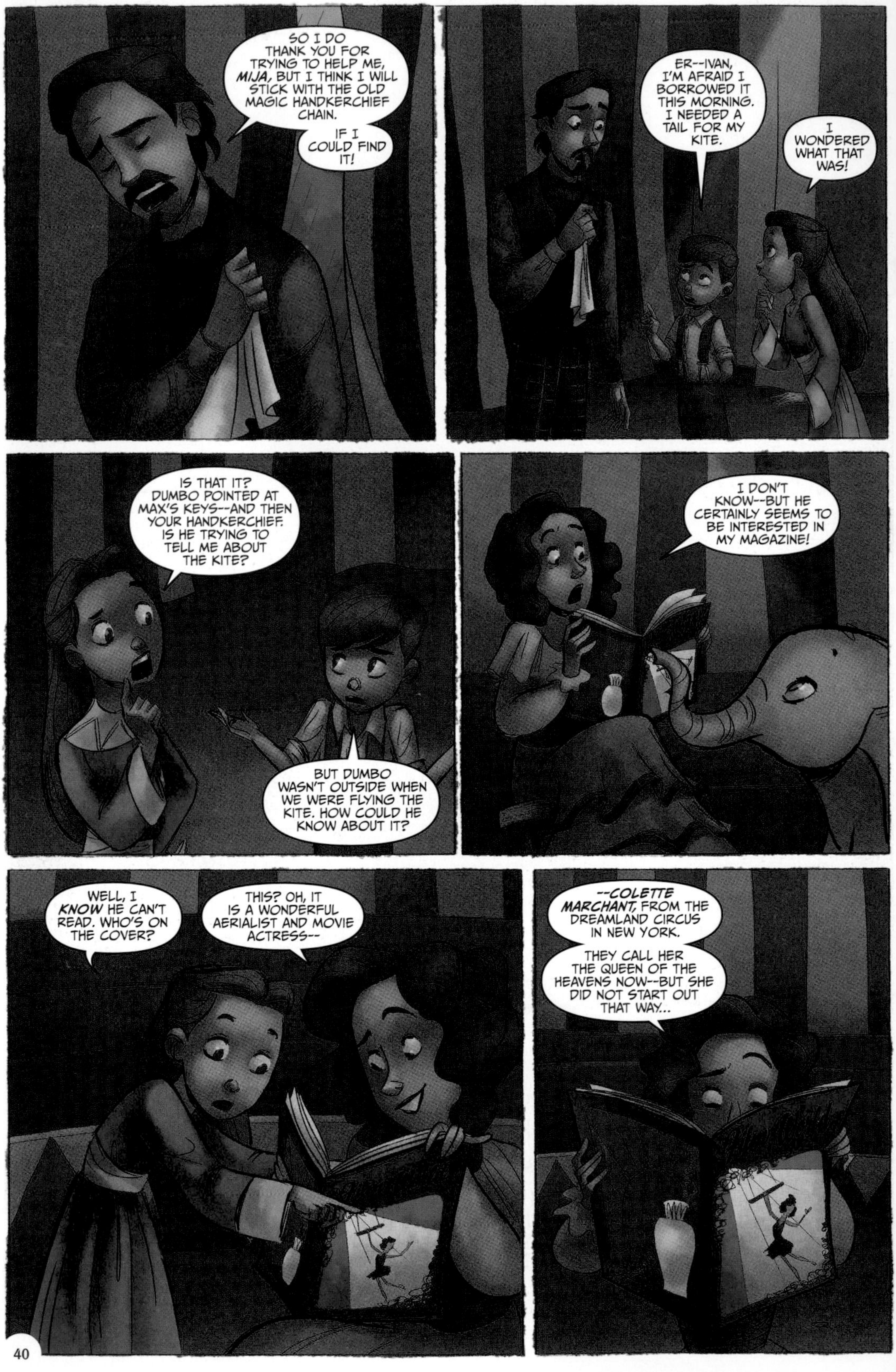
SO I DO THANK YOU FOR TRYING TO HELP ME, MIJA, BUT I THINK I WILL STICK WITH THE OLD MAGIC HANDKERCHIEF CHAIN.
IF I COULD FIND IT!
ER--IVAN, I'M AFRAID I BORROWED IT THIS MORNING. I NEEDED A TAIL FOR MY KITE.
I WONDERED WHAT THAT WAS!
IS THAT IT? DUMBO POINTED AT MAX'S KEYS--AND THEN YOUR HANDKERCHIEF. IS HE TRYING TO TELL ME ABOUT THE KITE?
BUT DUMBO WASN'T OUTSIDE WHEN WE WERE FLYING THE KITE. HOW COULD HE KNOW ABOUT IT?
I DON'T KNOW--BUT HE CERTAINLY SEEMS TO BE INTERESTED IN MY MAGAZINE!
WELL, I KNOW HE CAN'T READ. WHO'S ON THE COVER?
THIS? OH, IT IS A WONDERFUL AERIALIST AND MOVIE ACTRESS--
--COLETTE MARCHANT, FROM THE DREAMLAND CIRCUS IN NEW YORK.
THEY CALL HER THE QUEEN OF THE HEAVENS NOW--BUT SHE DID NOT START OUT THAT WAY...

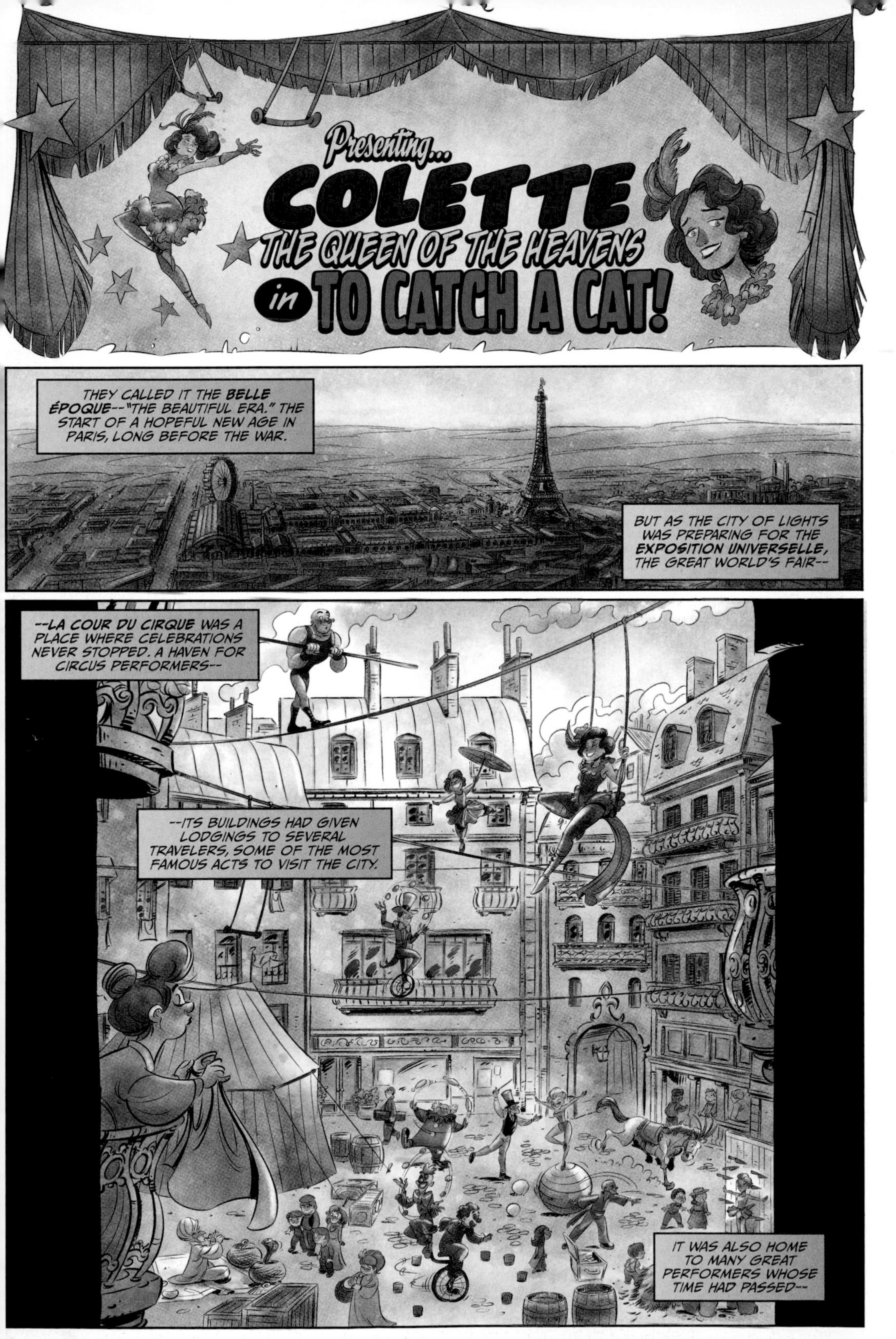
Presenting...
COLETTE
THE QUEEN OF THE HEAVENS
in TO CATCH A CAT!
THEY CALLED IT THE BELLE ÉPOQUE--"THE BEAUTIFUL ERA." THE START OF A HOPEFUL NEW AGE IN PARIS, LONG BEFORE THE WAR.
BUT AS THE CITY OF LIGHTS WAS PREPARING FOR THE EXPOSITION UNIVERSELLE, THE GREAT WORLD'S FAIR--
--LA COUR DU CIRQUE WAS A PLACE WHERE CELEBRATIONS NEVER STOPPED. A HAVEN FOR CIRCUS PERFORMERS--
--ITS BUILDINGS HAD GIVEN LODGINGS TO SEVERAL TRAVELERS, SOME OF THE MOST FAMOUS ACTS TO VISIT THE CITY.
IT WAS ALSO HOME TO MANY GREAT PERFORMERS WHOSE TIME HAD PASSED--

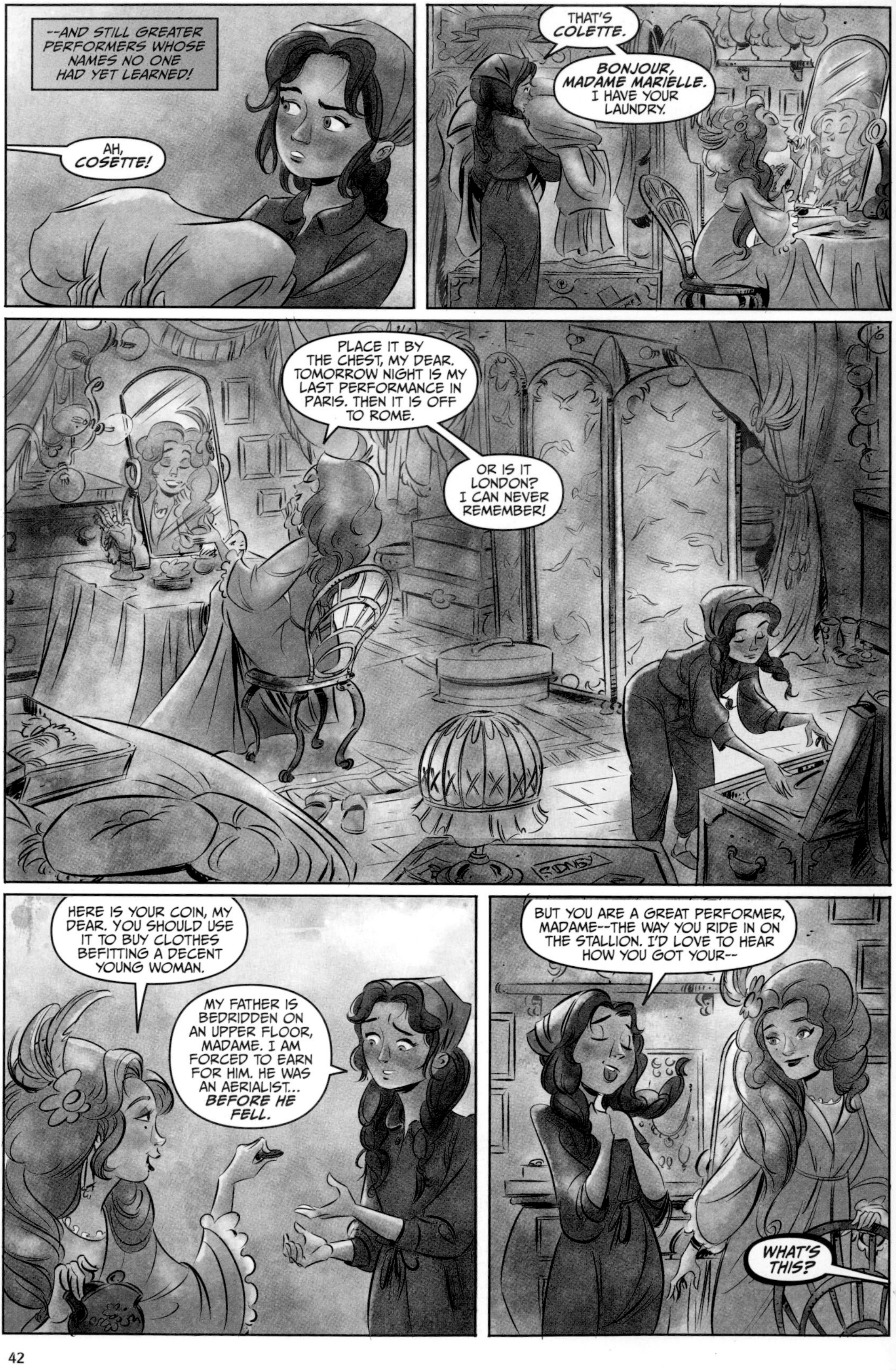
--AND STILL GREATER PERFORMERS WHOSE NAMES NO ONE HAD YET LEARNED!
AH, COSETTE!
THAT'S COLETTE.
BONJOUR, MADAME MARIELLE. I HAVE YOUR LAUNDRY.
PLACE IT BY THE CHEST, MY DEAR. TOMORROW NIGHT IS MY LAST PERFORMANCE IN PARIS. THEN IT IS OFF TO ROME.
OR IS IT LONDON? I CAN NEVER REMEMBER!
HERE IS YOUR COIN, MY DEAR. YOU SHOULD USE IT TO BUY CLOTHES BEFITTING A DECENT YOUNG WOMAN.
MY FATHER IS BEDRIDDEN ON AN UPPER FLOOR, MADAME. I AM FORCED TO EARN FOR HIM. HE WAS AN AERIALIST... BEFORE HE FELL.
BUT YOU ARE A GREAT PERFORMER, MADAME--THE WAY YOU RIDE IN ON THE STALLION. I'D LOVE TO HEAR HOW YOU GOT YOUR--
WHAT'S THIS?

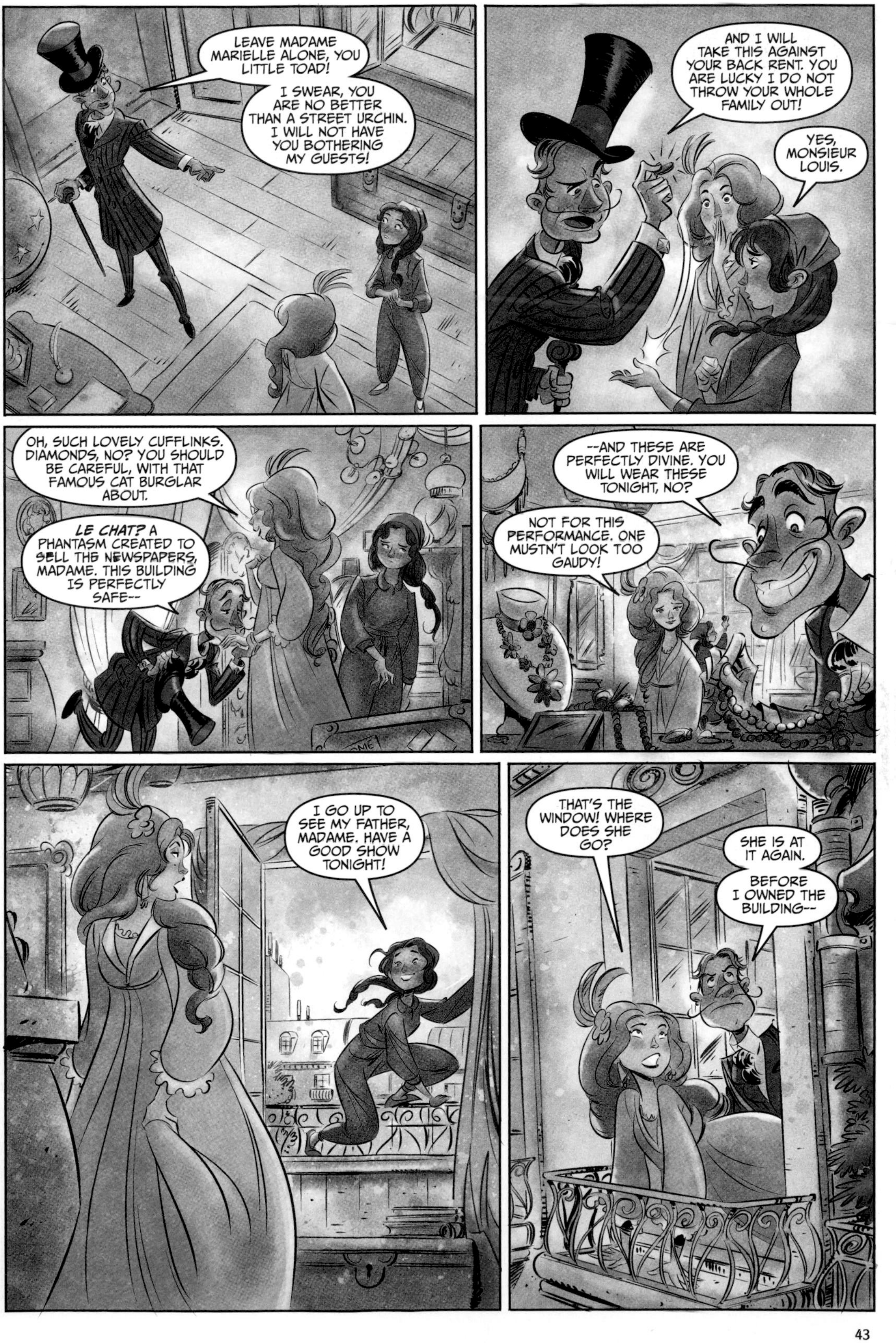
LEAVE MADAME MARIELLE ALONE, YOU LITTLE TOAD!
I SWEAR, YOU ARE NO BETTER THAN A STREET URCHIN. I WILL NOT HAVE YOU BOTHERING MY GUESTS!
AND I WILL TAKE THIS AGAINST YOUR BACK RENT. YOU ARE LUCKY I DO NOT THROW YOUR WHOLE FAMILY OUT!
YES, MONSIEUR LOUIS.
OH, SUCH LOVELY CUFFLINKS. DIAMONDS, NO? YOU SHOULD BE CAREFUL, WITH THAT FAMOUS CAT BURGLAR ABOUT.
LE CHAT? A PHANTASM CREATED TO SELL THE NEWSPAPERS, MADAME. THIS BUILDING IS PERFECTLY SAFE--
--AND THESE ARE PERFECTLY DIVINE. YOU WILL WEAR THESE TONIGHT, NO?
NOT FOR THIS PERFORMANCE. ONE MUSTN'T LOOK TOO GAUDY!
I GO UP TO SEE MY FATHER, MADAME. HAVE A GOOD SHOW TONIGHT!
THAT'S THE WINDOW! WHERE DOES SHE GO?
SHE IS AT IT AGAIN.
BEFORE I OWNED THE BUILDING--

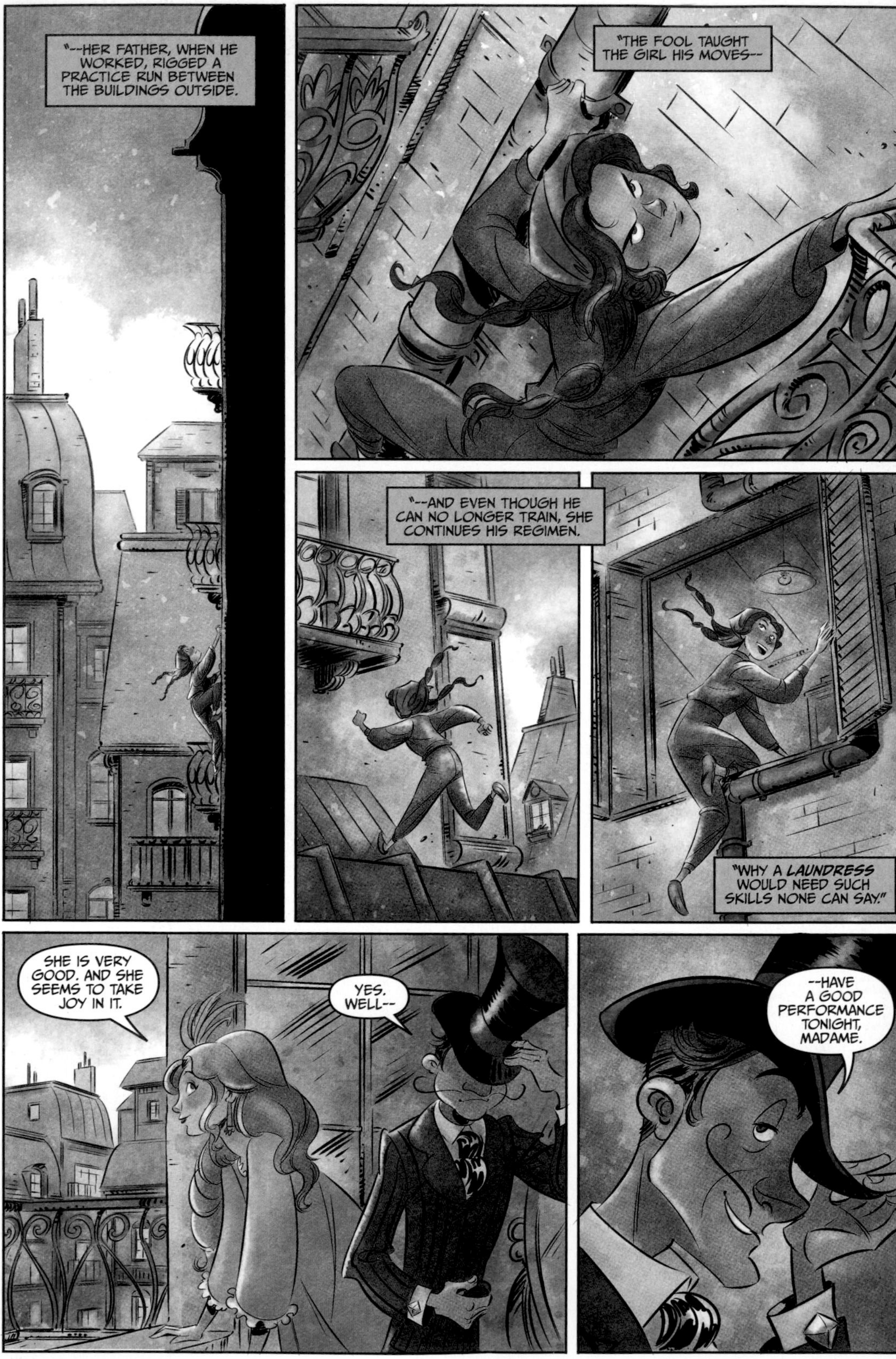
"--HER FATHER, WHEN HE WORKED, RIGGED A PRACTICE RUN BETWEEN THE BUILDINGS OUTSIDE.
"THE FOOL TAUGHT THE GIRL HIS MOVES--
"--AND EVEN THOUGH HE CAN NO LONGER TRAIN, SHE CONTINUES HIS REGIMEN.
"WHY A *LAUNDRESS* WOULD NEED SUCH SKILLS NONE CAN SAY."
SHE IS VERY GOOD. AND SHE SEEMS TO TAKE JOY IN IT.
YES. WELL--
--HAVE A GOOD PERFORMANCE TONIGHT, MADAME.

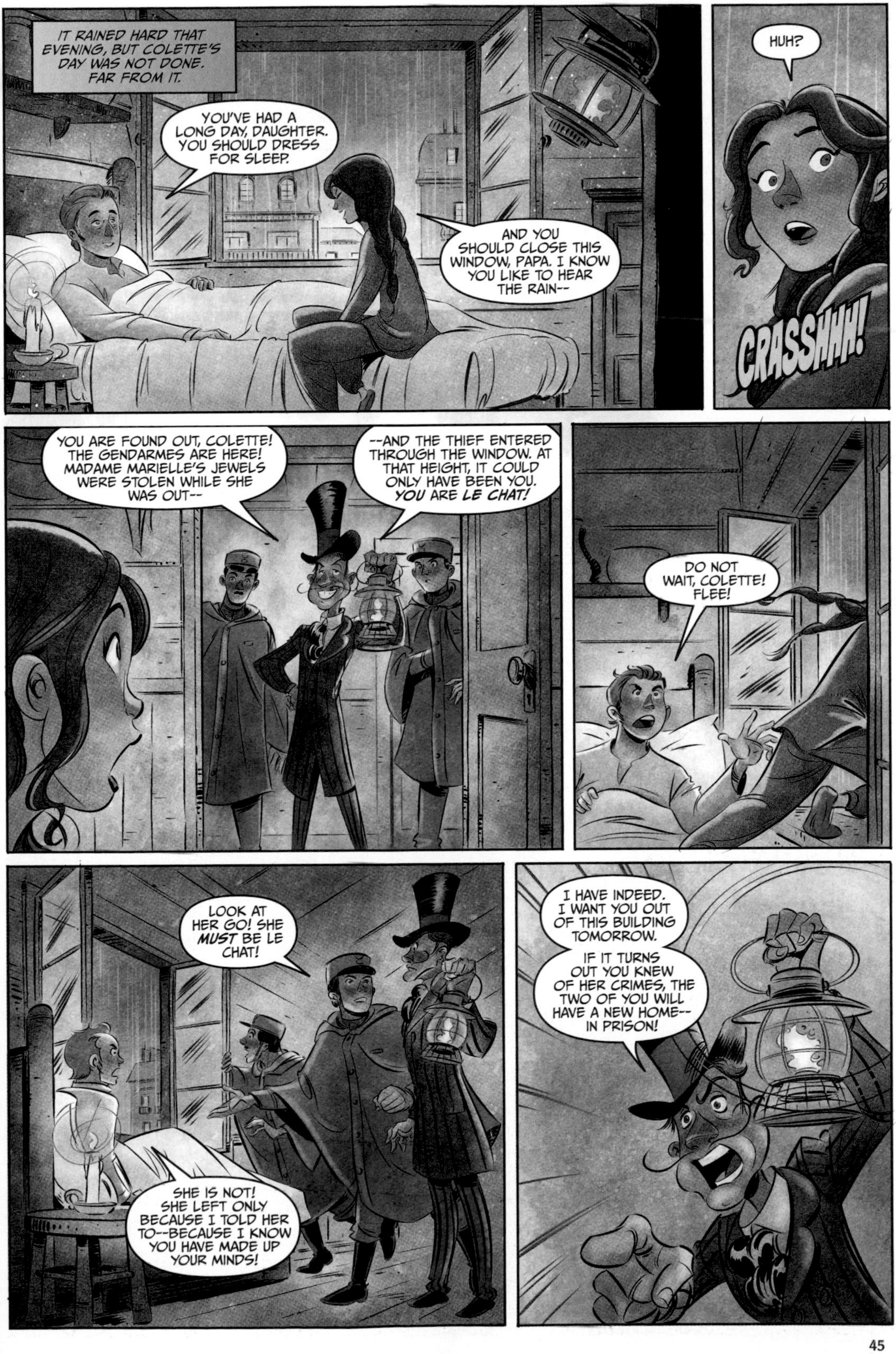
IT RAINED HARD THAT EVENING, BUT COLETTE'S DAY WAS NOT DONE. FAR FROM IT.
YOU'VE HAD A LONG DAY, DAUGHTER. YOU SHOULD DRESS FOR SLEEP.
AND YOU SHOULD CLOSE THIS WINDOW, PAPA. I KNOW YOU LIKE TO HEAR THE RAIN--
HUH?
CRASSHHH!
YOU ARE FOUND OUT, COLETTE! THE GENDARMES ARE HERE! MADAME MARIELLE'S JEWELS WERE STOLEN WHILE SHE WAS OUT--
--AND THE THIEF ENTERED THROUGH THE WINDOW. AT THAT HEIGHT, IT COULD ONLY HAVE BEEN YOU. YOU ARE LE CHAT!
DO NOT WAIT, COLETTE! FLEE!
LOOK AT HER GO! SHE MUST BE LE CHAT!
SHE IS NOT! SHE LEFT ONLY BECAUSE I TOLD HER TO--BECAUSE I KNOW YOU HAVE MADE UP YOUR MINDS!
I HAVE INDEED. I WANT YOU OUT OF THIS BUILDING TOMORROW.
IF IT TURNS OUT YOU KNEW OF HER CRIMES, THE TWO OF YOU WILL HAVE A NEW HOME-- IN PRISON!

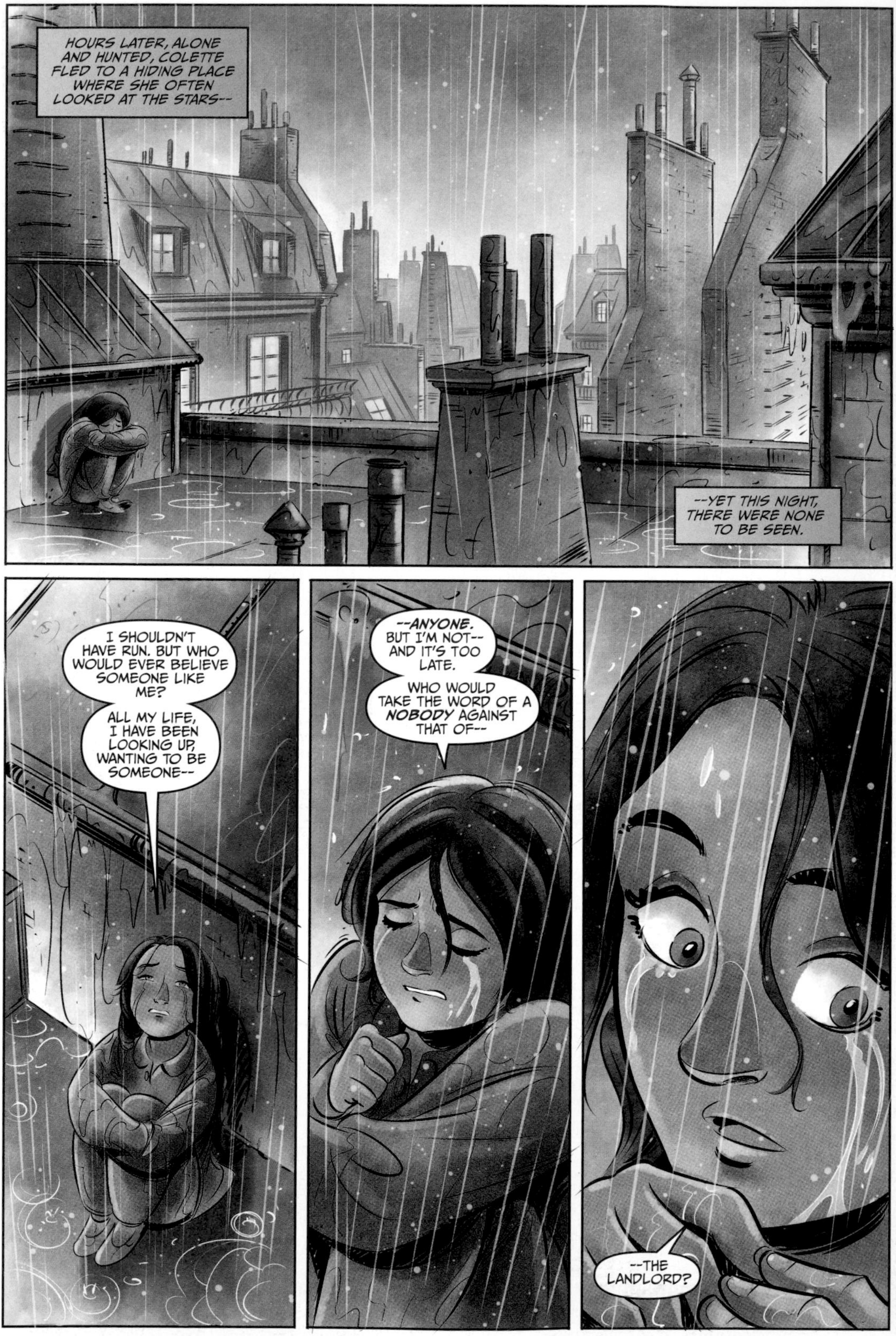
HOURS LATER, ALONE AND HUNTED, COLETTE FLED TO A HIDING PLACE WHERE SHE OFTEN LOOKED AT THE STARS--
--YET THIS NIGHT, THERE WERE NONE TO BE SEEN.
I SHOULDN'T HAVE RUN. BUT WHO WOULD EVER BELIEVE SOMEONE LIKE ME?
ALL MY LIFE, I HAVE BEEN LOOKING UP, WANTING TO BE SOMEONE--
--ANYONE. BUT I'M NOT-- AND IT'S TOO LATE.
WHO WOULD TAKE THE WORD OF A NOBODY AGAINST THAT OF--
--THE LANDLORD?

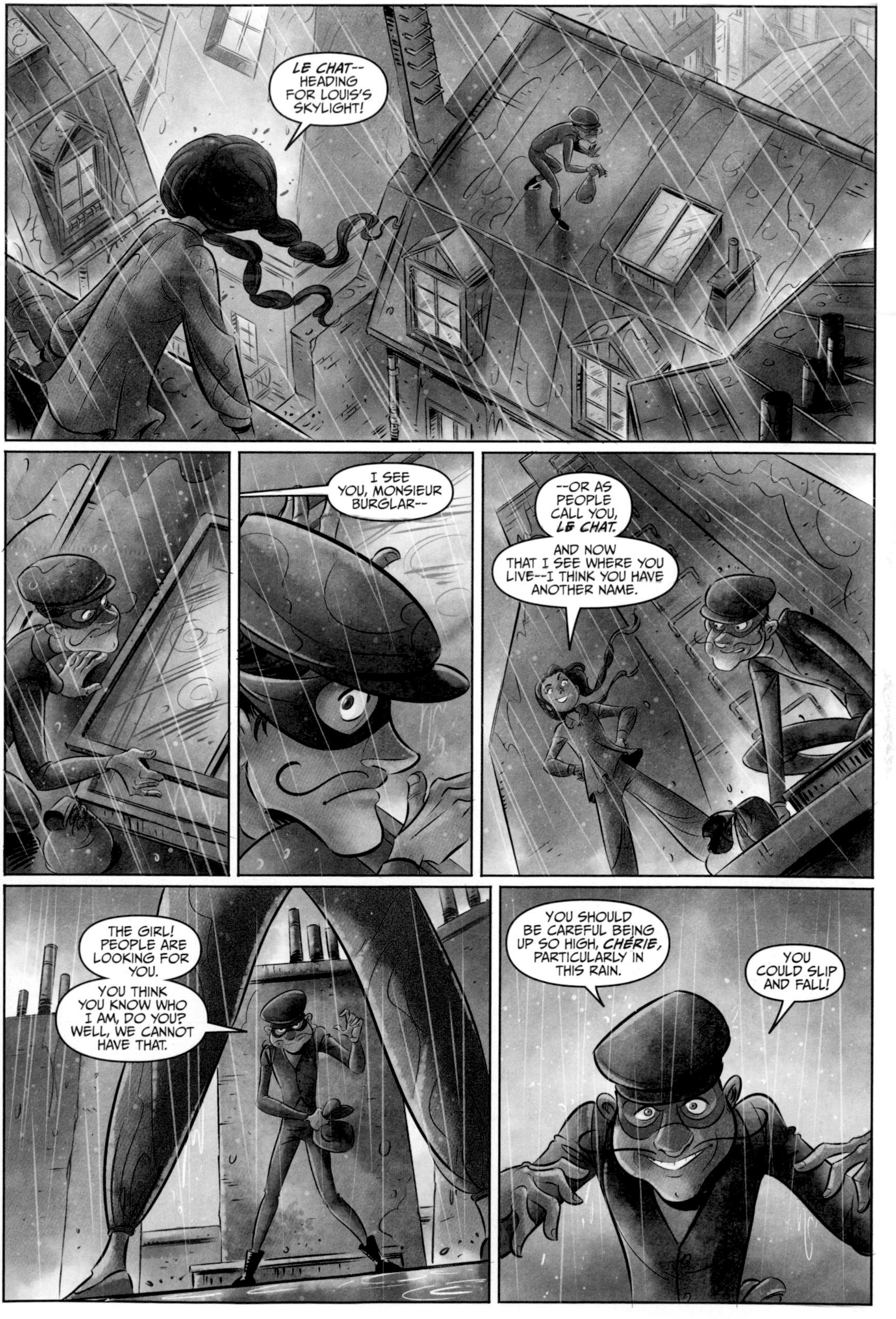
LE CHAT--
HEADING FOR LOUIS'S SKYLIGHT!
I SEE YOU, MONSIEUR BURGLAR--
--OR AS PEOPLE CALL YOU, LE CHAT.
AND NOW THAT I SEE WHERE YOU LIVE--I THINK YOU HAVE ANOTHER NAME.
THE GIRL! PEOPLE ARE LOOKING FOR YOU.
YOU THINK YOU KNOW WHO I AM, DO YOU? WELL, WE CANNOT HAVE THAT.
YOU SHOULD BE CAREFUL BEING UP SO HIGH, CHÉRIE, PARTICULARLY IN THIS RAIN.
YOU COULD SLIP AND FALL!

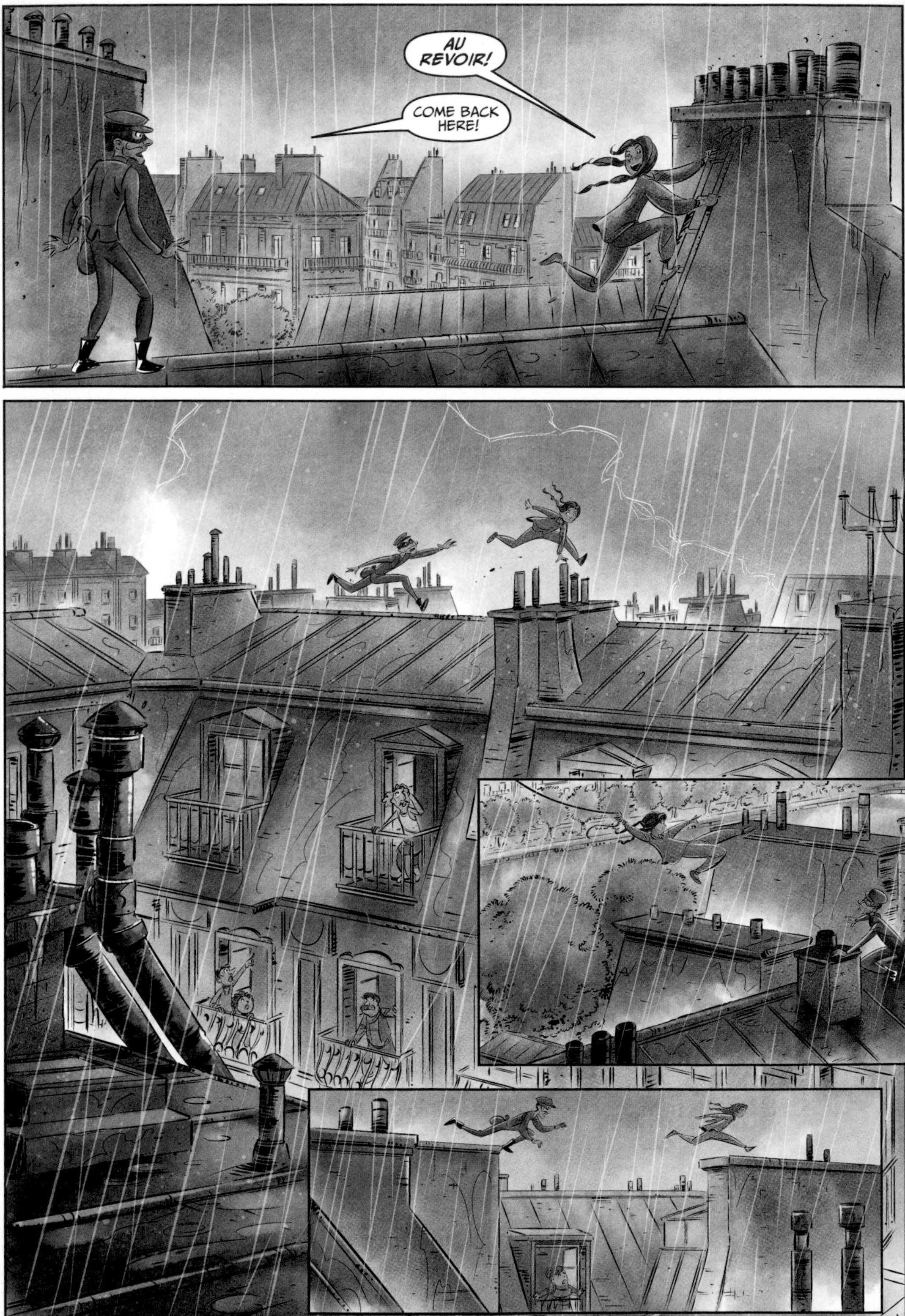
AU REVOIR!
COME BACK HERE!

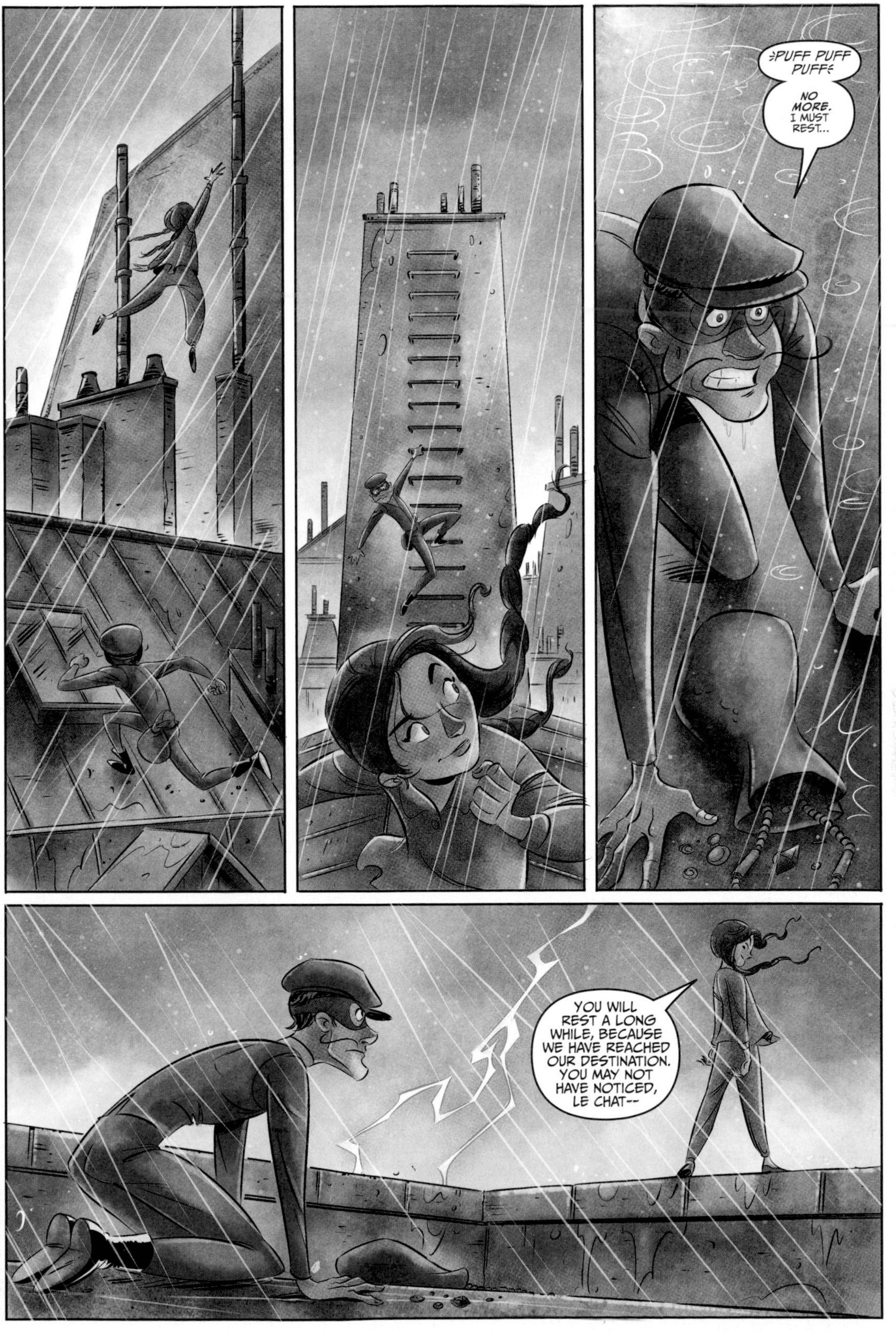
PUFF PUFF PUFF
NO MORE. I MUST REST...
YOU WILL REST A LONG WHILE, BECAUSE WE HAVE REACHED OUR DESTINATION. YOU MAY NOT HAVE NOTICED, LE CHAT--

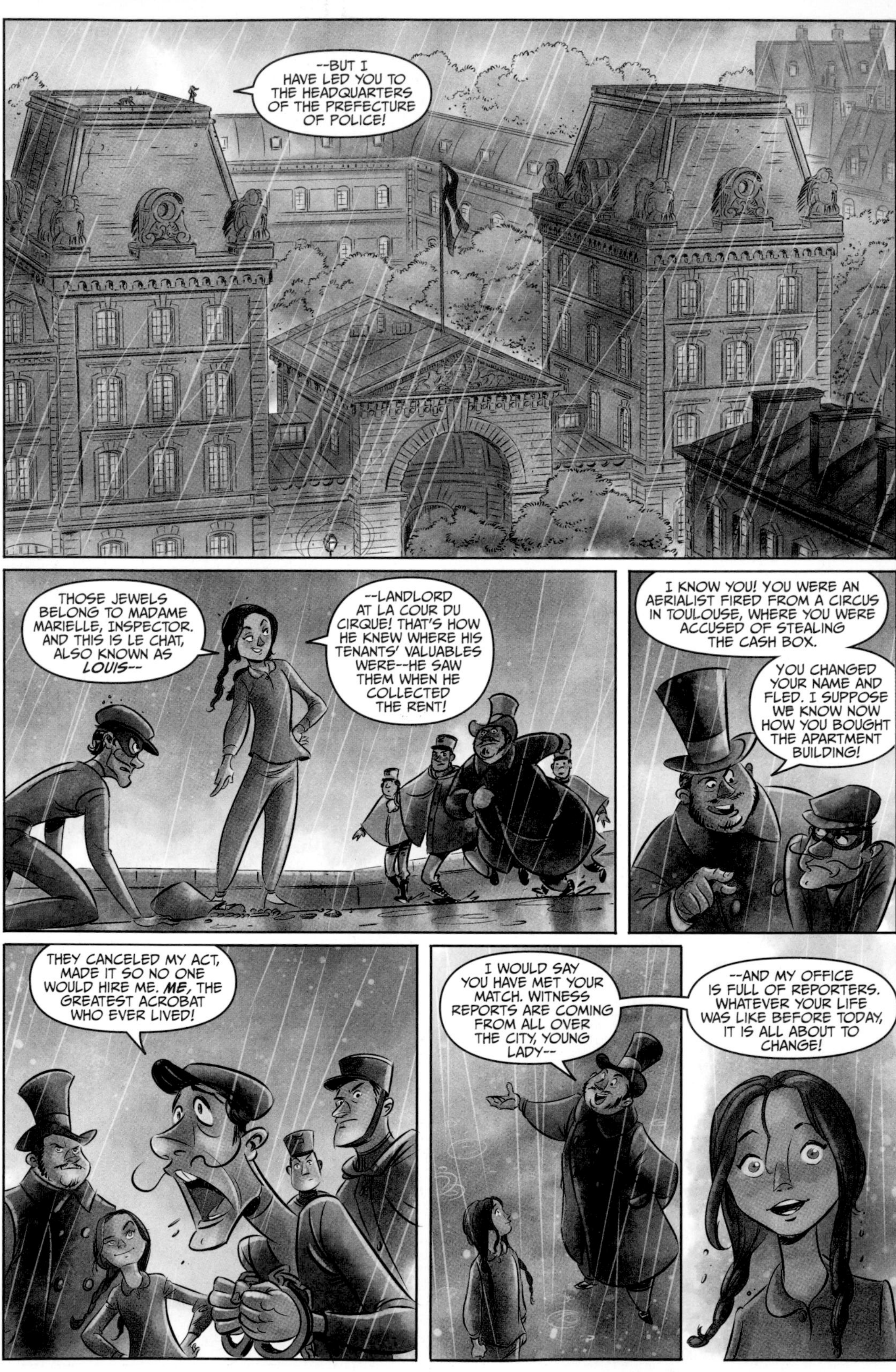
--BUT I HAVE LED YOU TO THE HEADQUARTERS OF THE PREFECTURE OF POLICE!
THOSE JEWELS BELONG TO MADAME MARIELLE, INSPECTOR. AND THIS IS LE CHAT, ALSO KNOWN AS *LOUIS*--
--LANDLORD AT LA COUR DU CIRQUE! THAT'S HOW HE KNEW WHERE HIS TENANTS' VALUABLES WERE--HE SAW THEM WHEN HE COLLECTED THE RENT!
I KNOW YOU! YOU WERE AN AERIALIST FIRED FROM A CIRCUS IN TOULOUSE, WHERE YOU WERE ACCUSED OF STEALING THE CASH BOX.
YOU CHANGED YOUR NAME AND FLED. I SUPPOSE WE KNOW NOW HOW YOU BOUGHT THE APARTMENT BUILDING!
THEY CANCELED MY ACT, MADE IT SO NO ONE WOULD HIRE ME. ***ME***, THE GREATEST ACROBAT WHO EVER LIVED!
I WOULD SAY YOU HAVE MET YOUR MATCH. WITNESS REPORTS ARE COMING FROM ALL OVER THE CITY, YOUNG LADY--
--AND MY OFFICE IS FULL OF REPORTERS. WHATEVER YOUR LIFE WAS LIKE BEFORE TODAY, IT IS ALL ABOUT TO CHANGE!

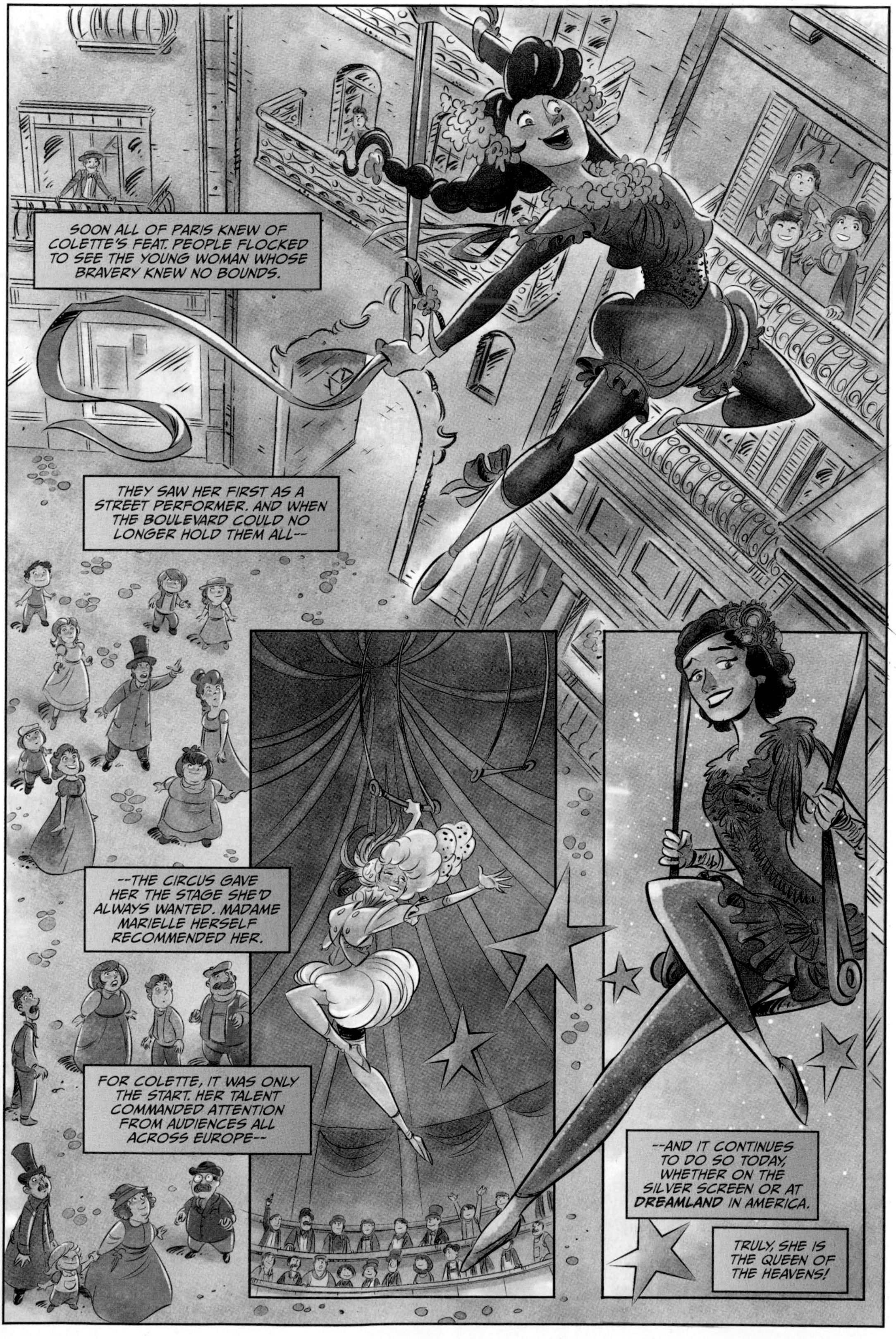
SOON ALL OF PARIS KNEW OF COLETTE'S FEAT. PEOPLE FLOCKED TO SEE THE YOUNG WOMAN WHOSE BRAVERY KNEW NO BOUNDS.
THEY SAW HER FIRST AS A STREET PERFORMER. AND WHEN THE BOULEVARD COULD NO LONGER HOLD THEM ALL--
--THE CIRCUS GAVE HER THE STAGE SHE'D ALWAYS WANTED. MADAME MARIELLE HERSELF RECOMMENDED HER.
FOR COLETTE, IT WAS ONLY THE START. HER TALENT COMMANDED ATTENTION FROM AUDIENCES ALL ACROSS EUROPE--
--AND IT CONTINUES TO DO SO TODAY, WHETHER ON THE SILVER SCREEN OR AT DREAMLAND IN AMERICA.
TRULY, SHE IS THE QUEEN OF THE HEAVENS!

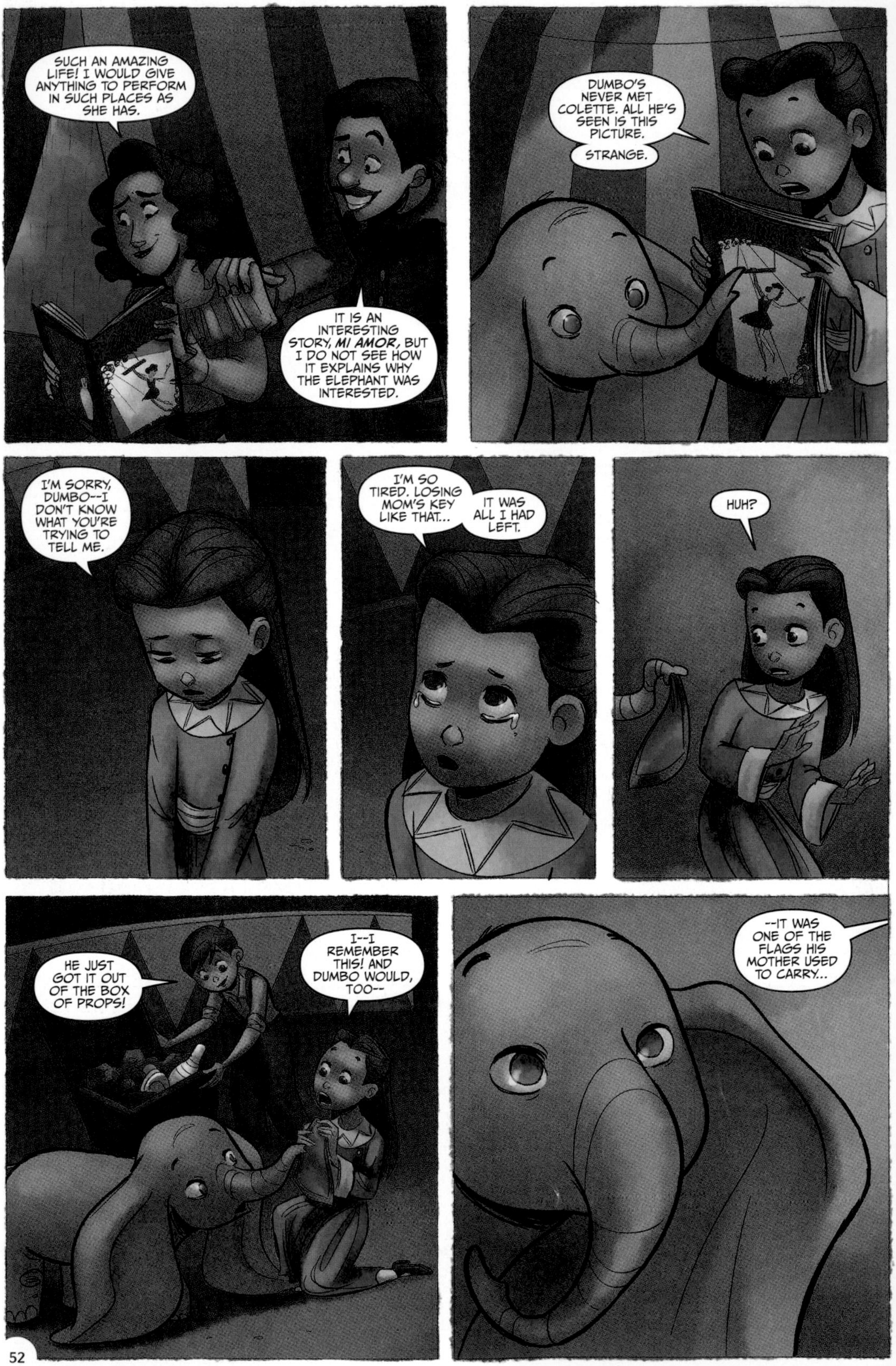
SUCH AN AMAZING LIFE! I WOULD GIVE ANYTHING TO PERFORM IN SUCH PLACES AS SHE HAS.
IT IS AN INTERESTING STORY, MI AMOR, BUT I DO NOT SEE HOW IT EXPLAINS WHY THE ELEPHANT WAS INTERESTED.
DUMBO'S NEVER MET COLETTE. ALL HE'S SEEN IS THIS PICTURE.
STRANGE.
I'M SORRY, DUMBO--I DON'T KNOW WHAT YOU'RE TRYING TO TELL ME.
I'M SO TIRED. LOSING MOM'S KEY LIKE THAT...
IT WAS ALL I HAD LEFT.
HUH?
HE JUST GOT IT OUT OF THE BOX OF PROPS!
I--I REMEMBER THIS! AND DUMBO WOULD, TOO--
--IT WAS ONE OF THE FLAGS HIS MOTHER USED TO CARRY...

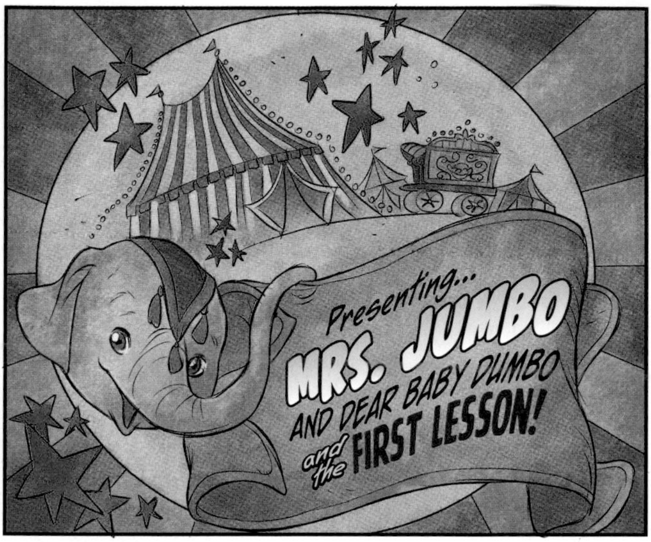
Presenting...
MRS. JUMBO
AND DEAR BABY DUMBO
and the FIRST LESSON!

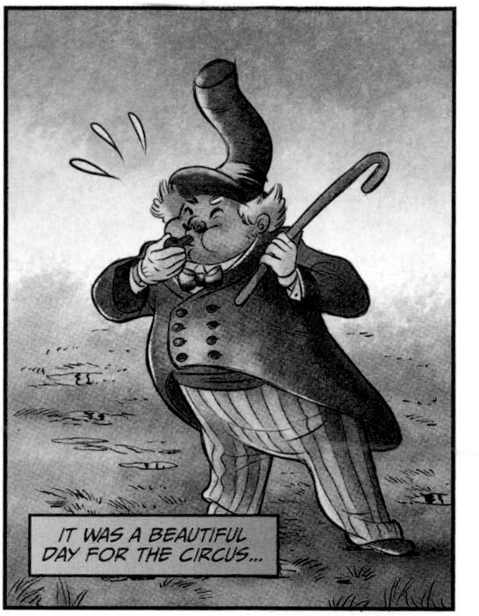
IT WAS A BEAUTIFUL DAY FOR THE CIRCUS...

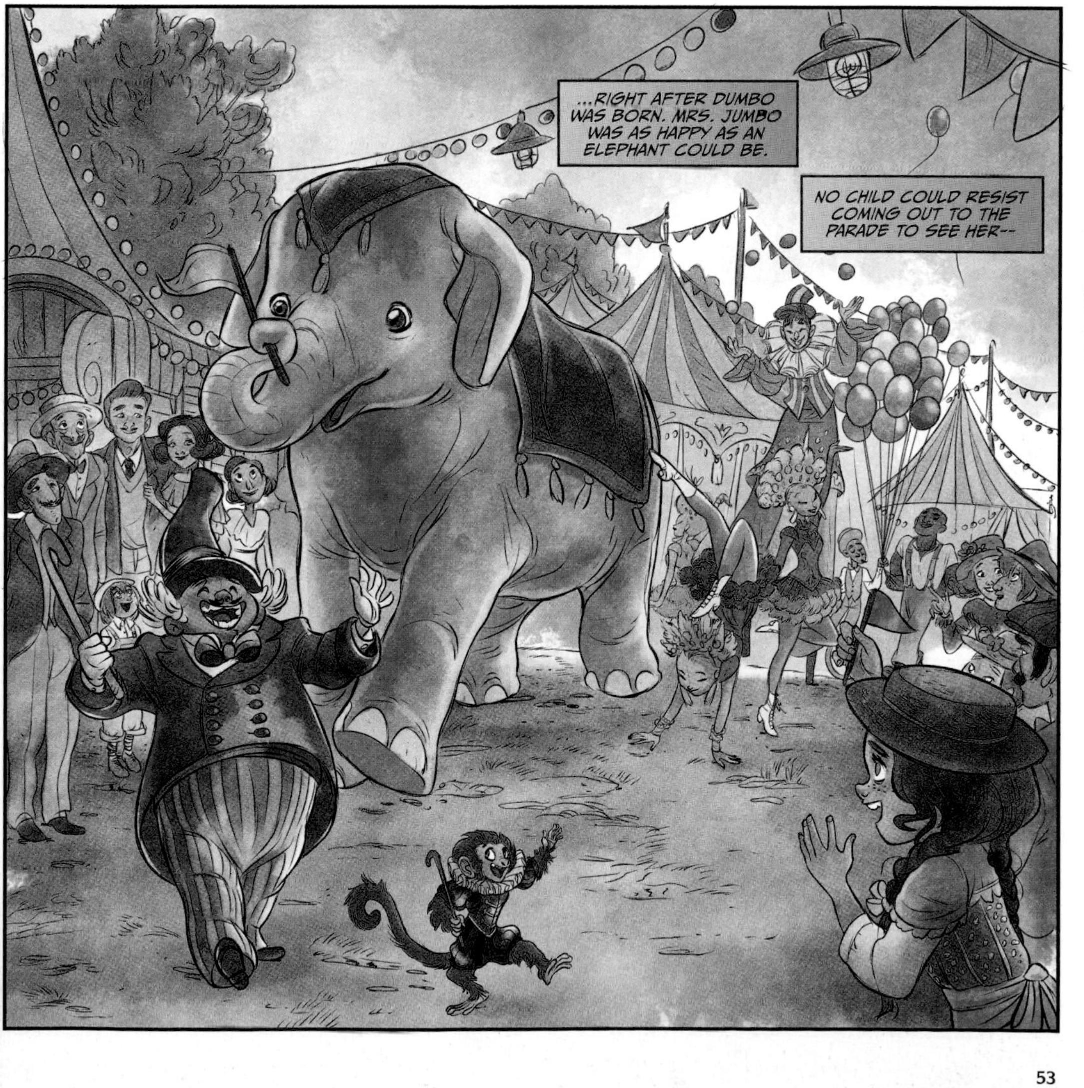
...RIGHT AFTER DUMBO WAS BORN. MRS. JUMBO WAS AS HAPPY AS AN ELEPHANT COULD BE.
NO CHILD COULD RESIST COMING OUT TO THE PARADE TO SEE HER--

--LEAST OF ALL, HER OWN!

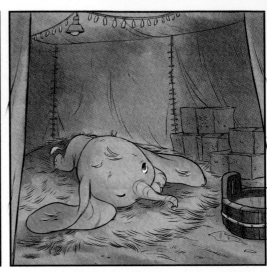

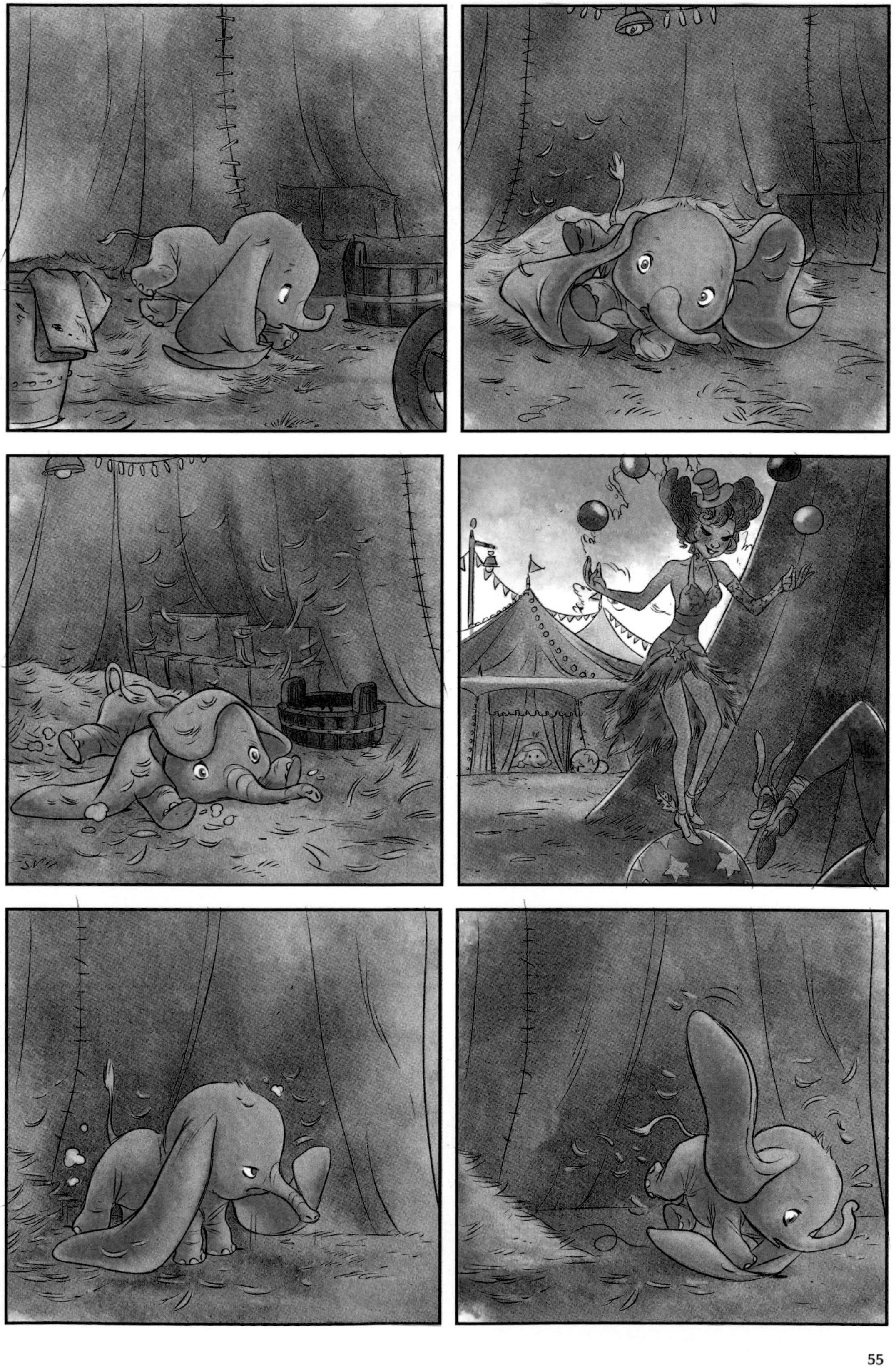

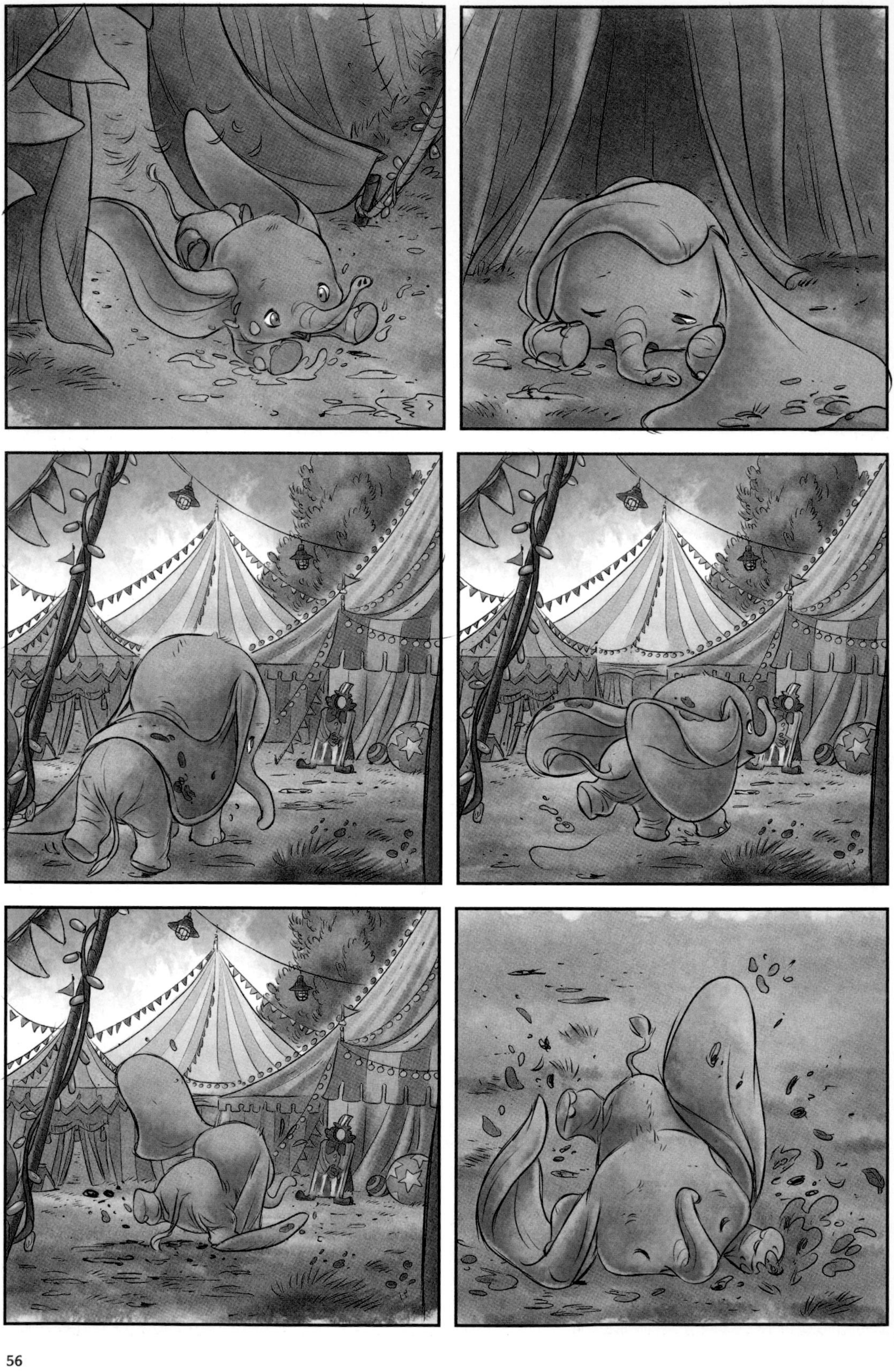

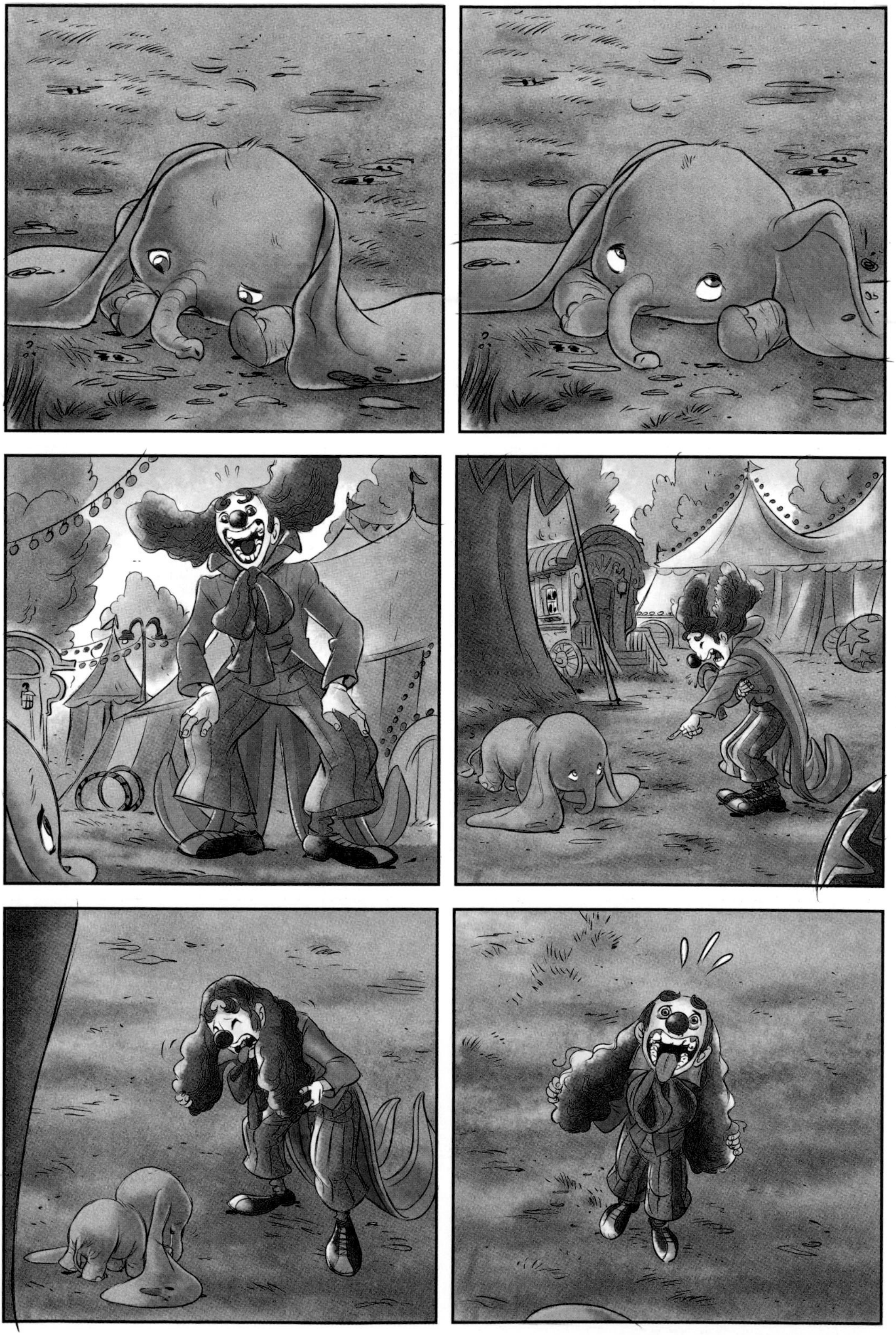

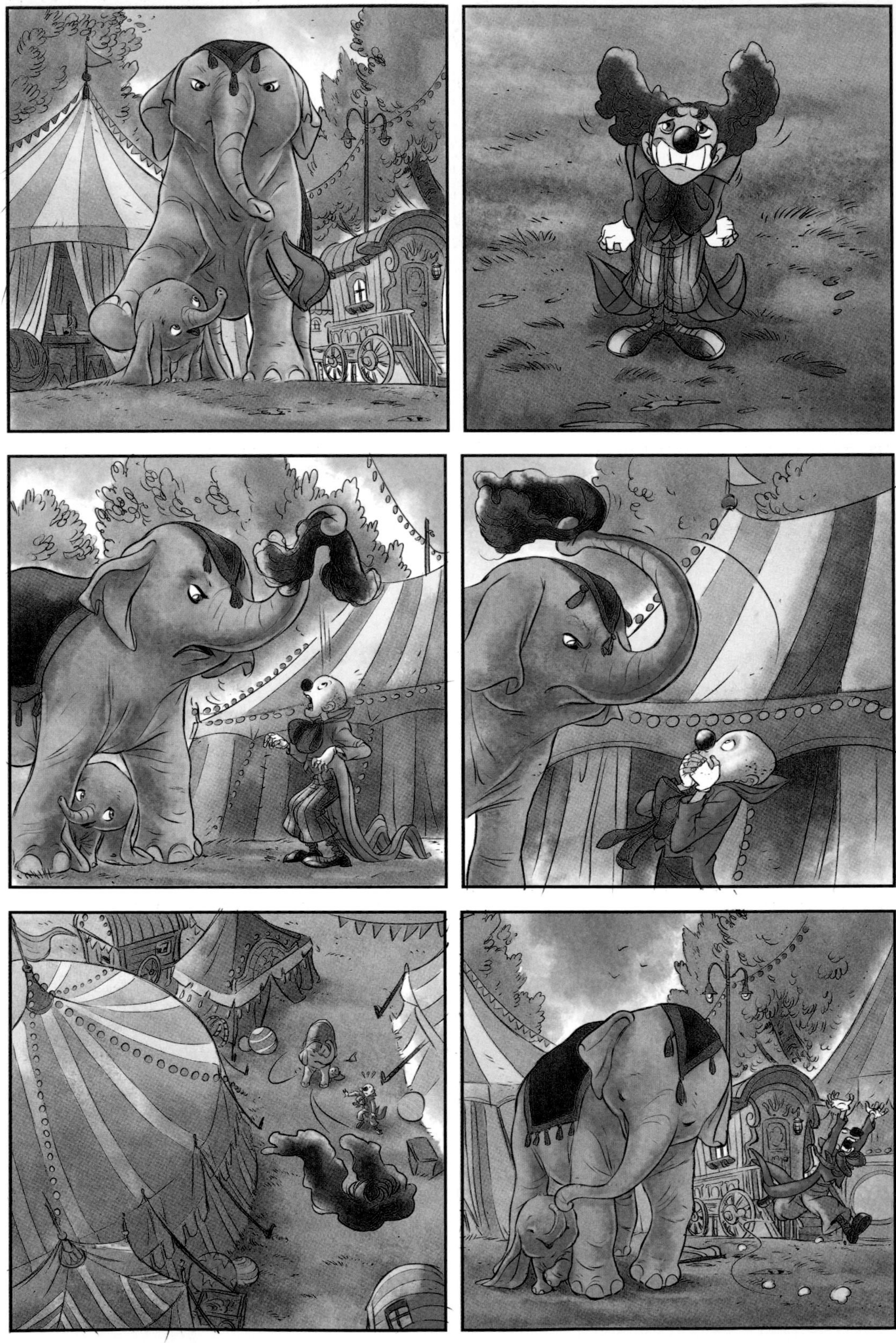

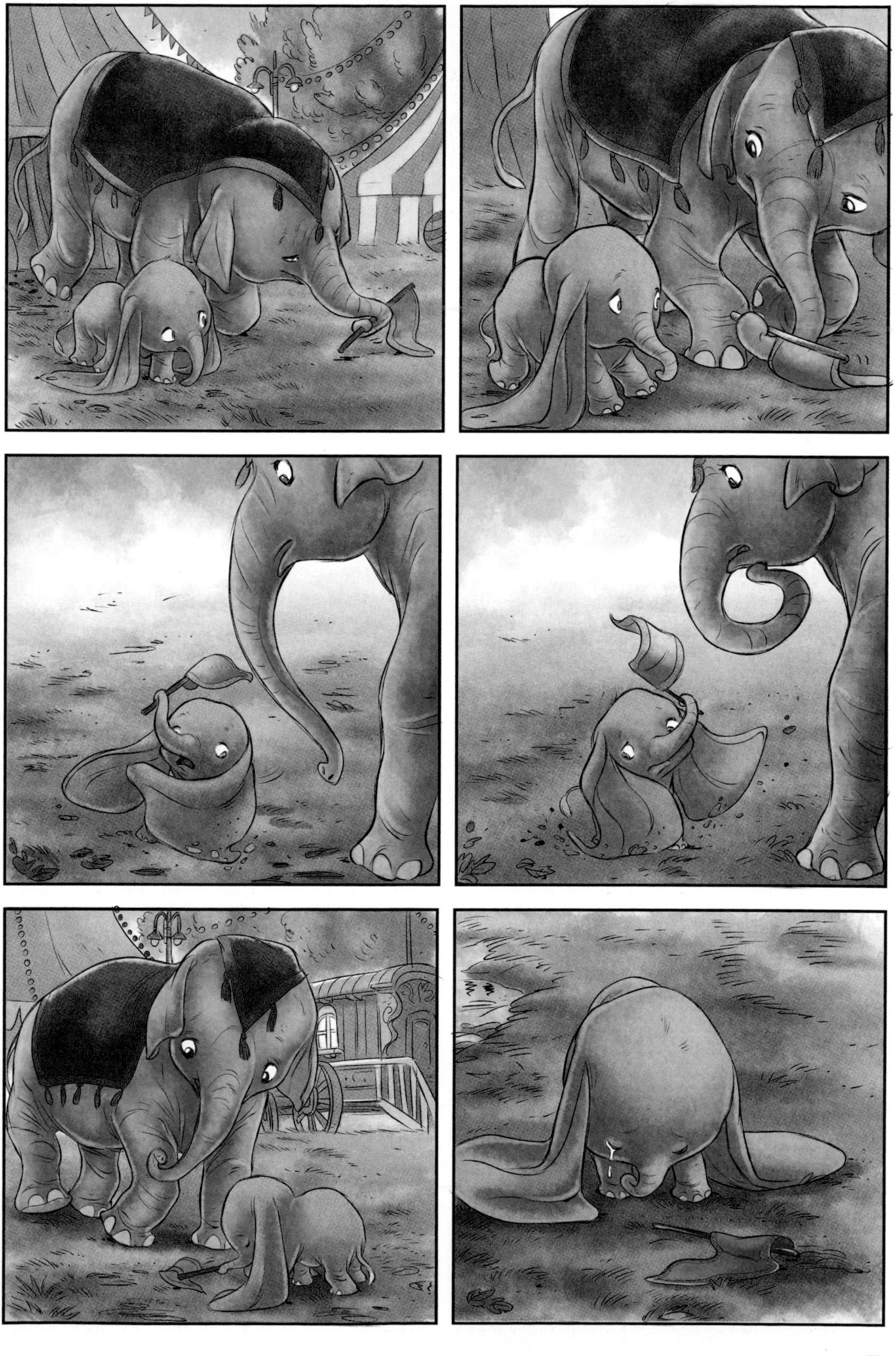

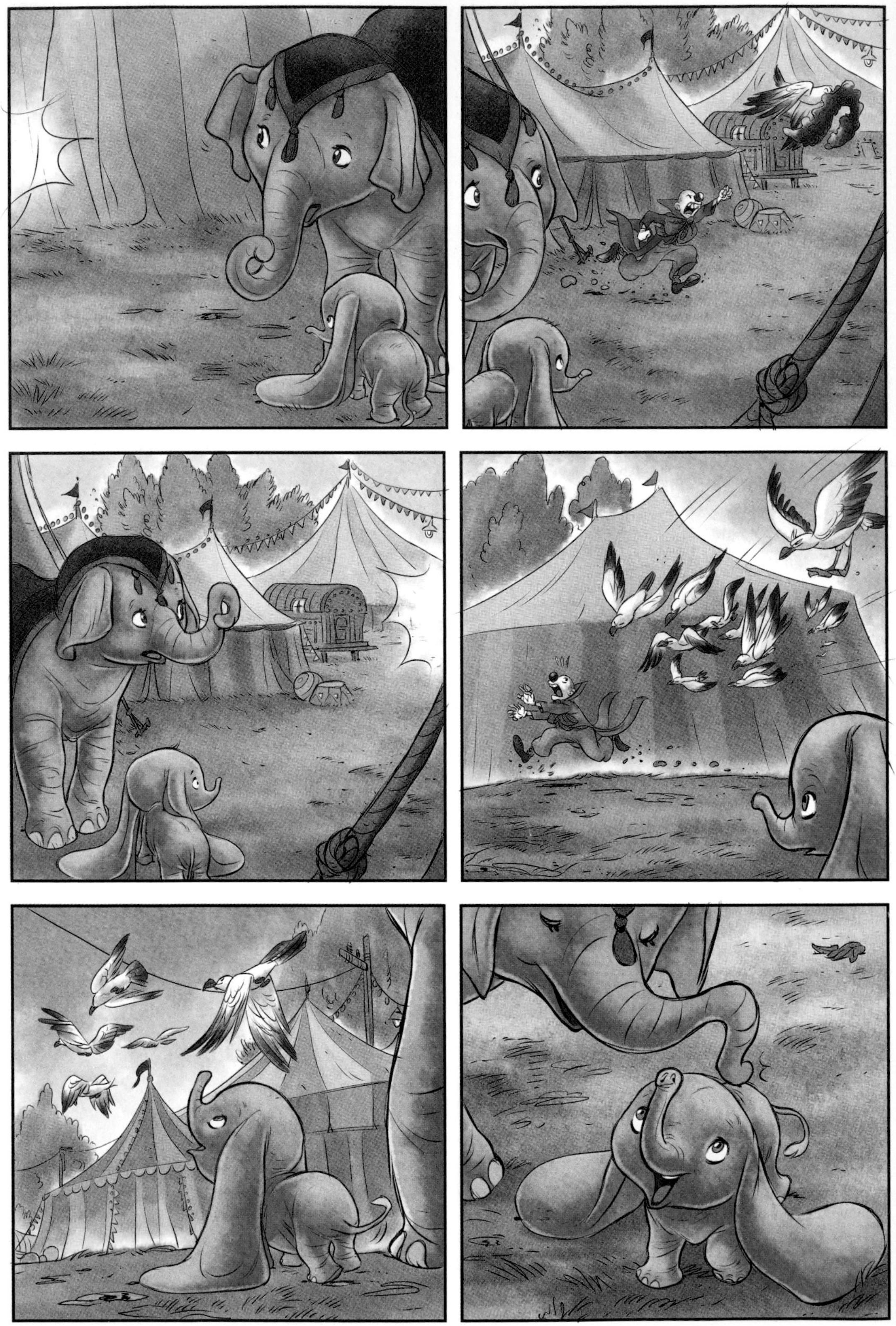

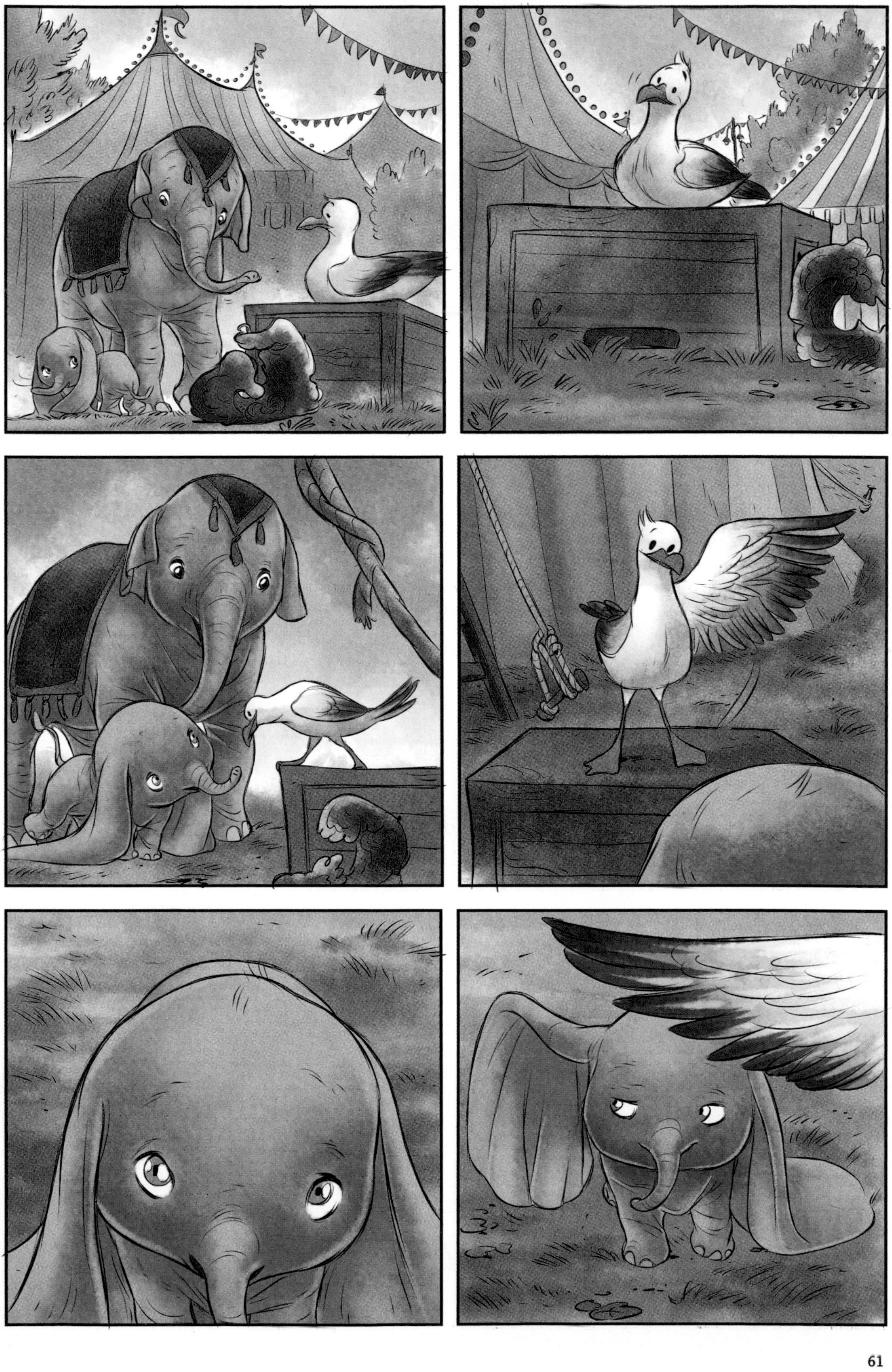

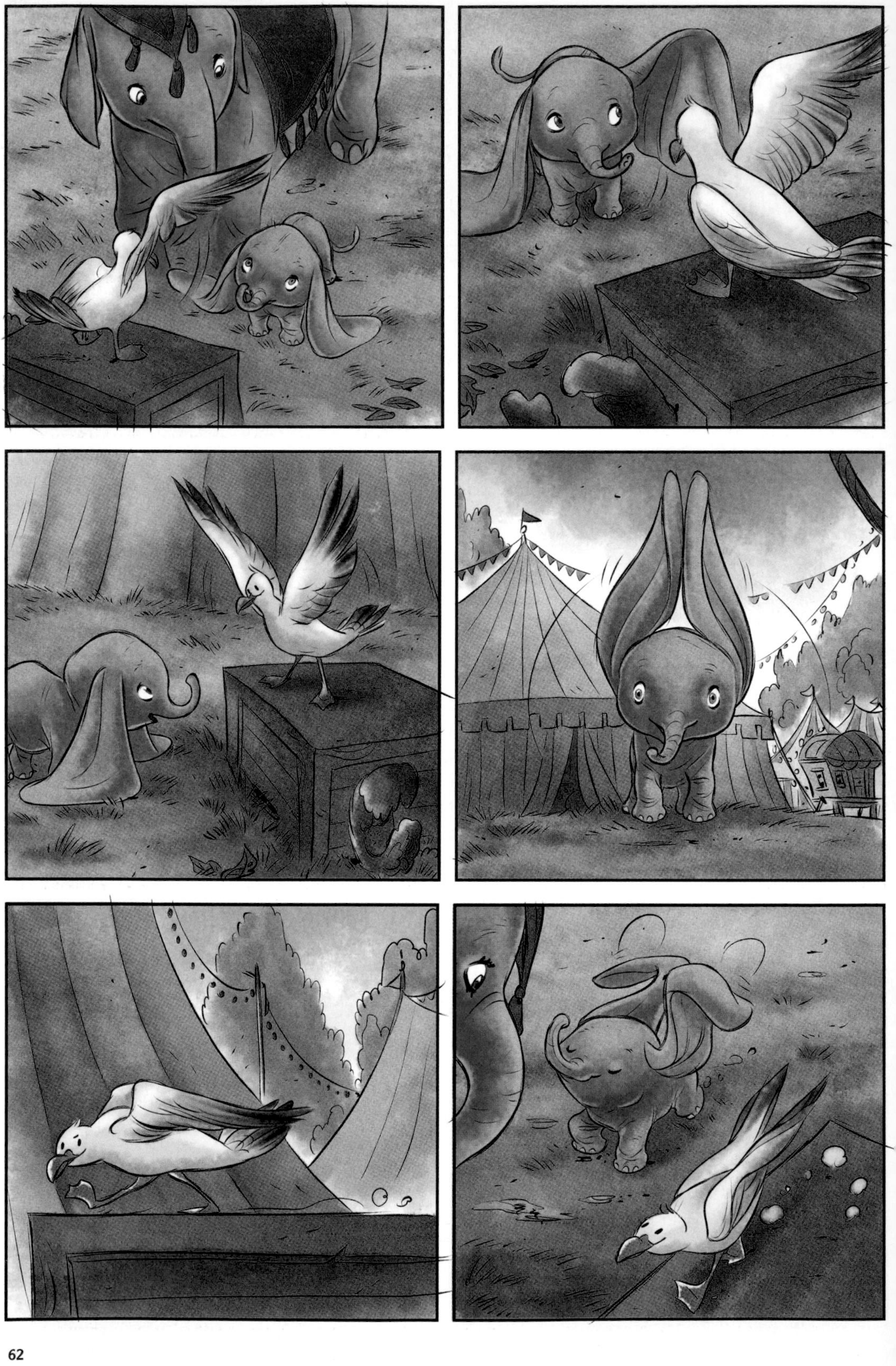

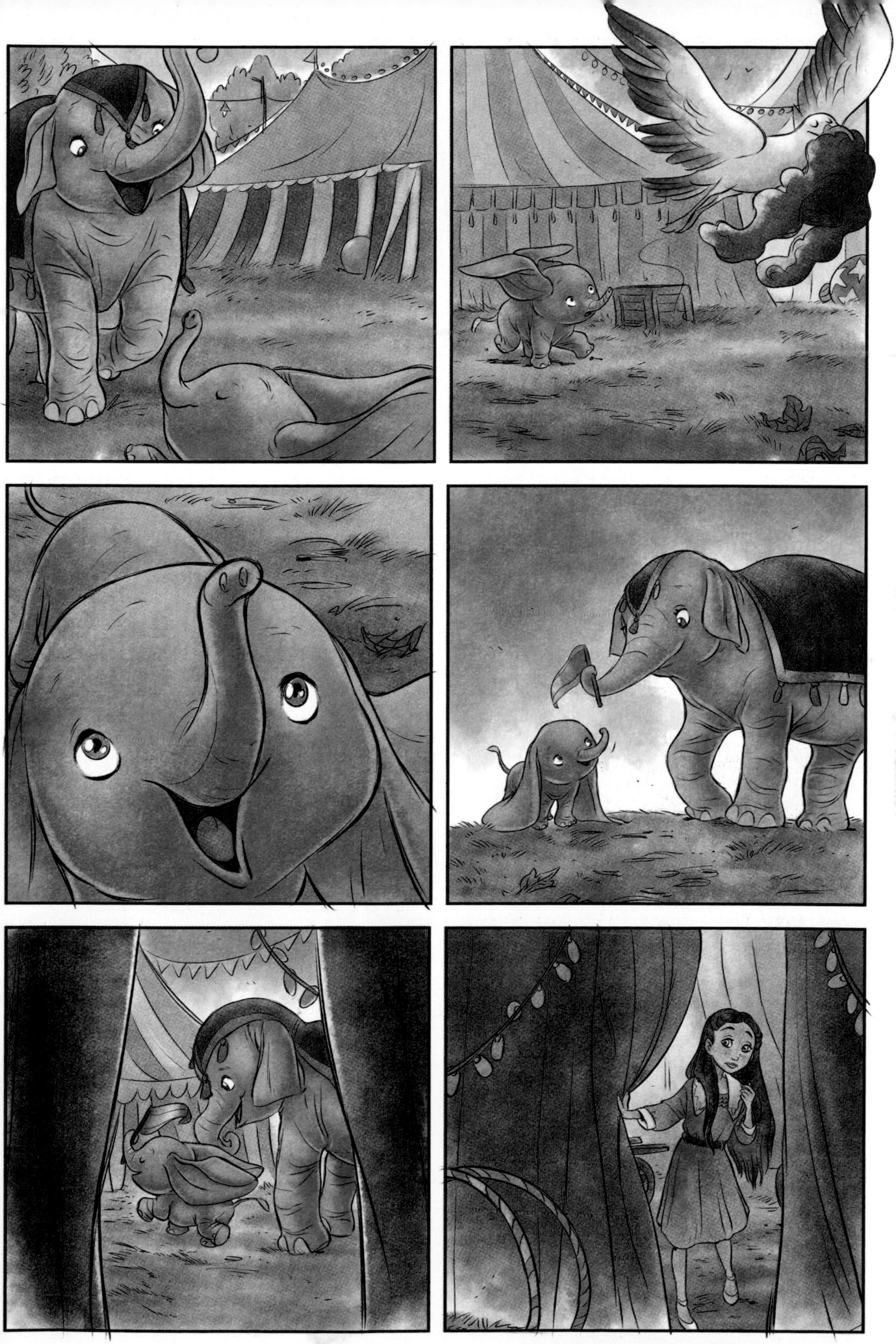

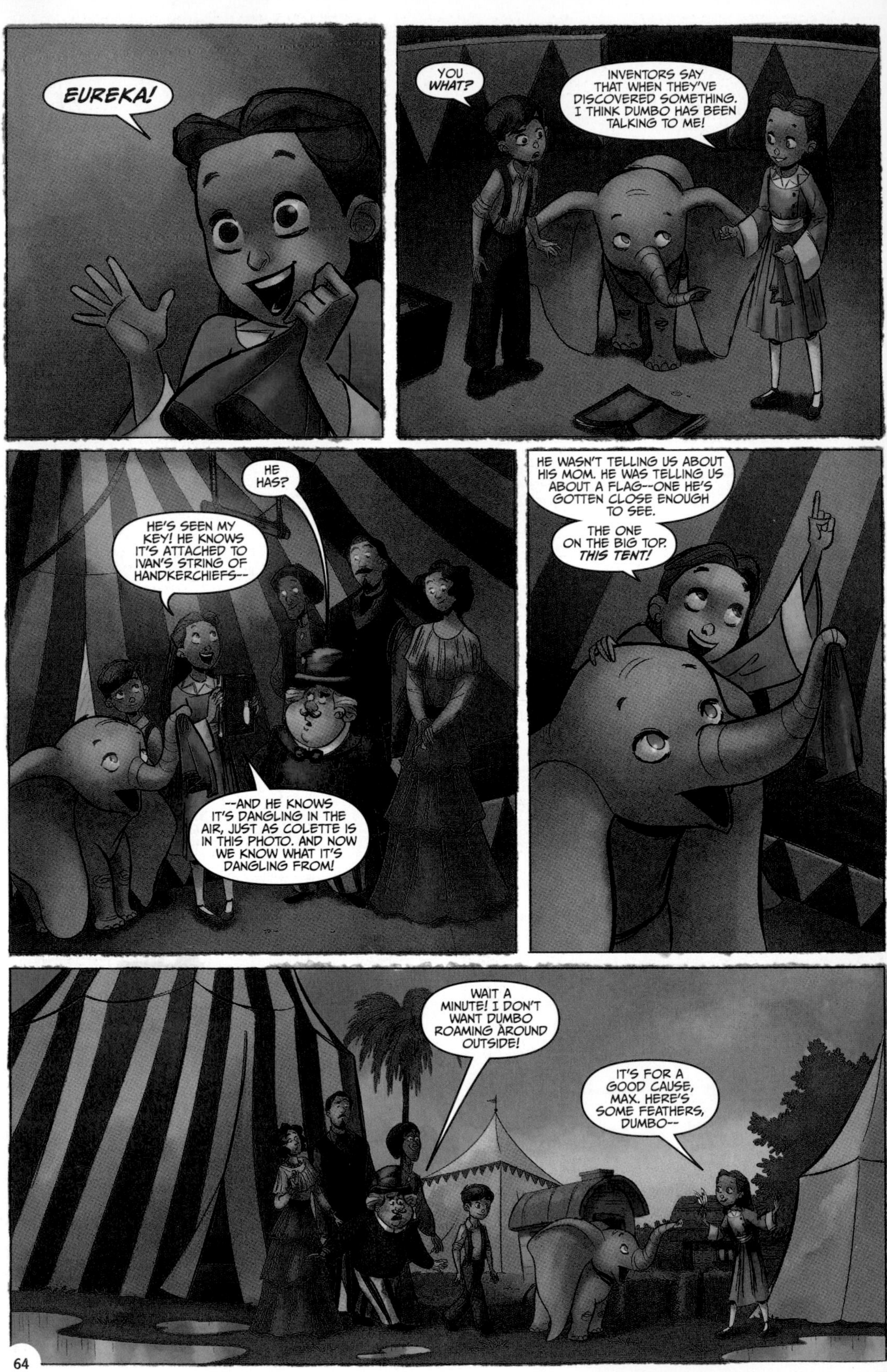
EUREKA!
YOU WHAT?
INVENTORS SAY THAT WHEN THEY'VE DISCOVERED SOMETHING. I THINK DUMBO HAS BEEN TALKING TO ME!
HE HAS?
HE'S SEEN MY KEY! HE KNOWS IT'S ATTACHED TO IVAN'S STRING OF HANDKERCHIEFS--
--AND HE KNOWS IT'S DANGLING IN THE AIR, JUST AS COLETTE IS IN THIS PHOTO. AND NOW WE KNOW WHAT IT'S DANGLING FROM!
HE WASN'T TELLING US ABOUT HIS MOM. HE WAS TELLING US ABOUT A FLAG--ONE HE'S GOTTEN CLOSE ENOUGH TO SEE.
THE ONE ON THE BIG TOP. THIS TENT!
WAIT A MINUTE! I DON'T WANT DUMBO ROAMING AROUND OUTSIDE!
IT'S FOR A GOOD CAUSE, MAX. HERE'S SOME FEATHERS, DUMBO--

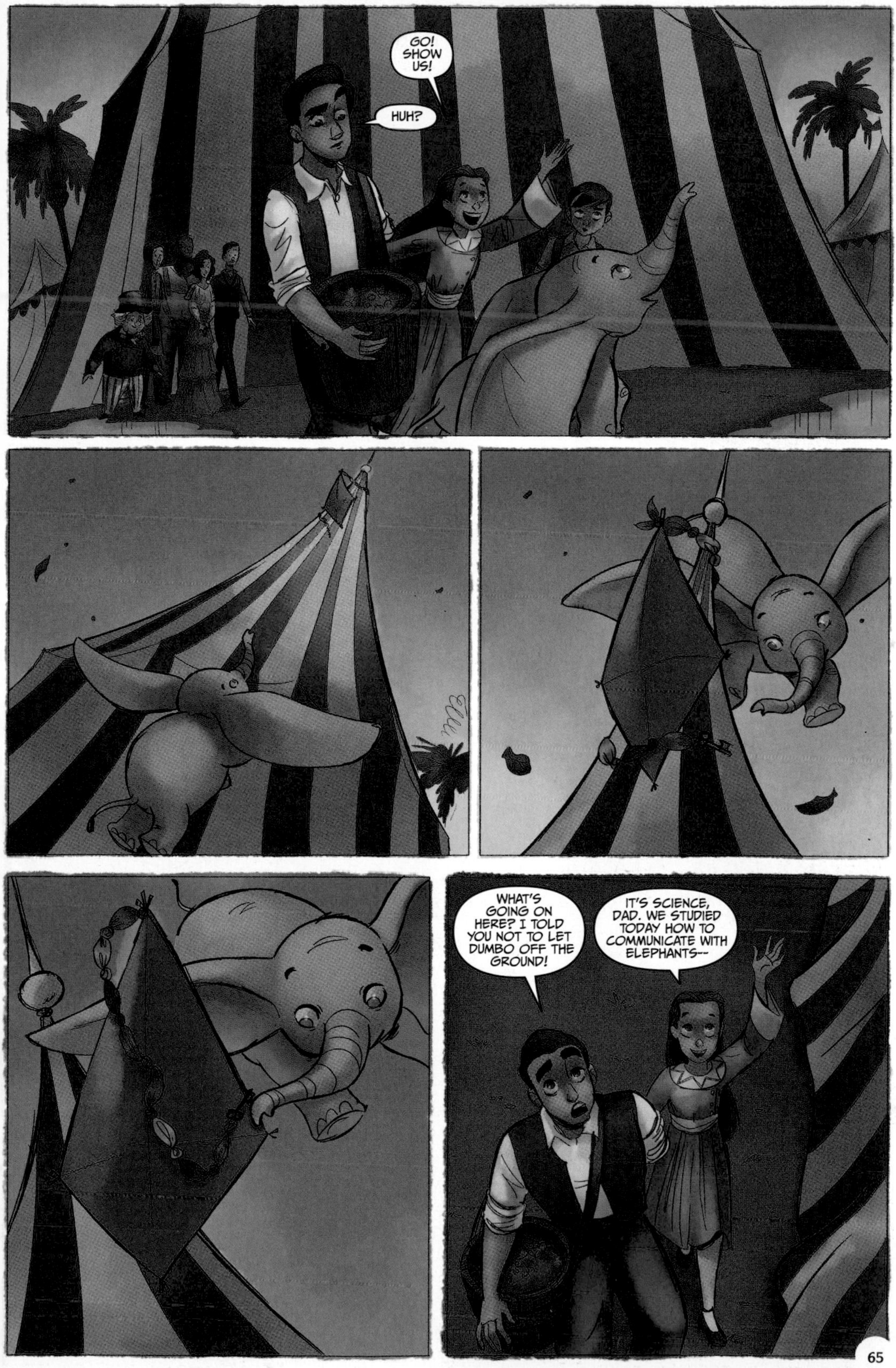
GO! SHOW US!
HUH?
WHAT'S GOING ON HERE? I TOLD YOU NOT TO LET DUMBO OFF THE GROUND!
IT'S SCIENCE, DAD. WE STUDIED TODAY HOW TO COMMUNICATE WITH ELEPHANTS--

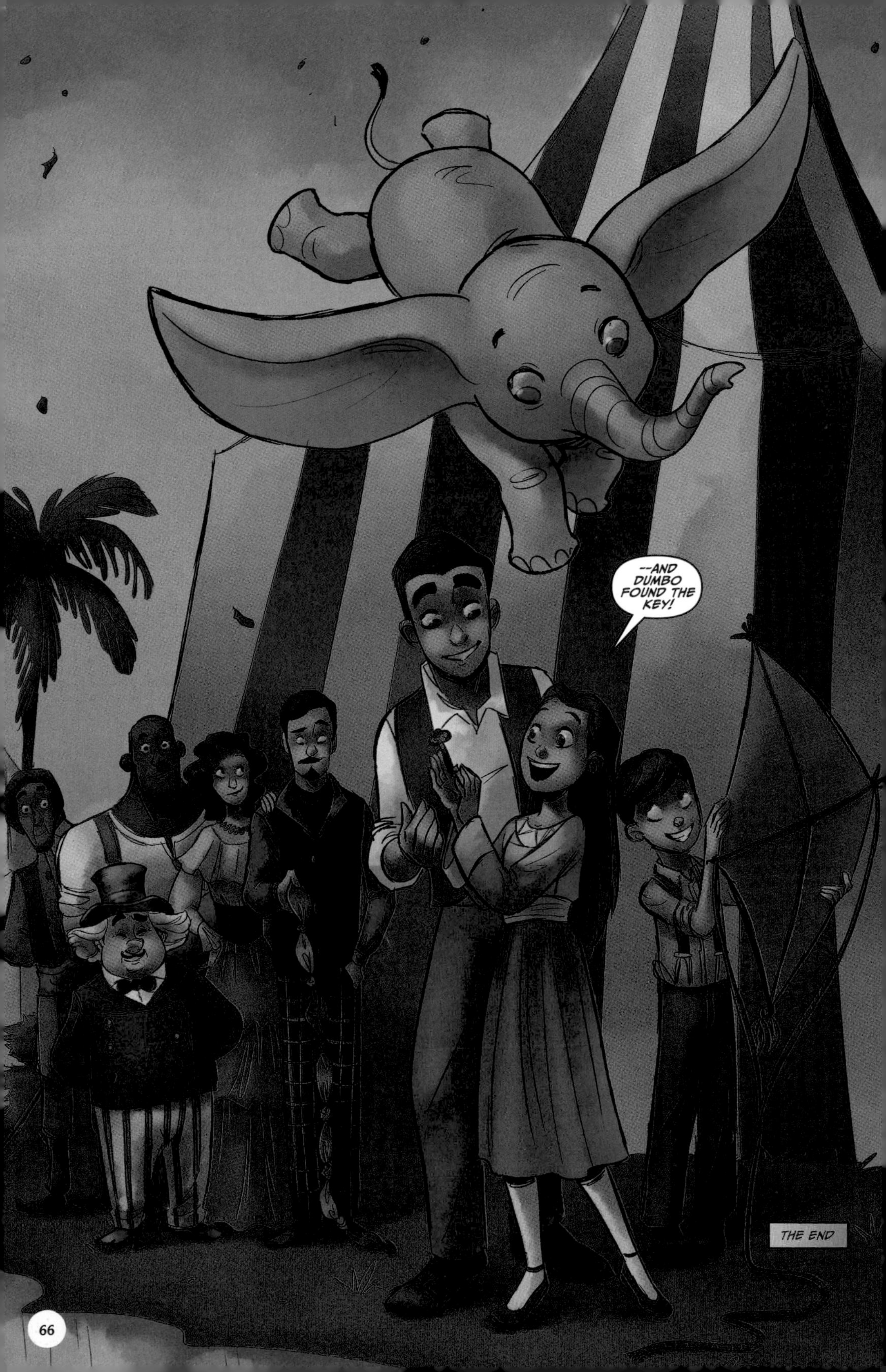
--AND DUMBO FOUND THE KEY!
THE END

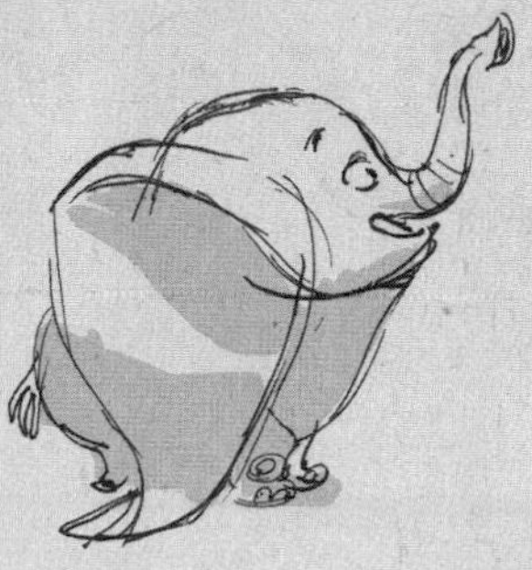

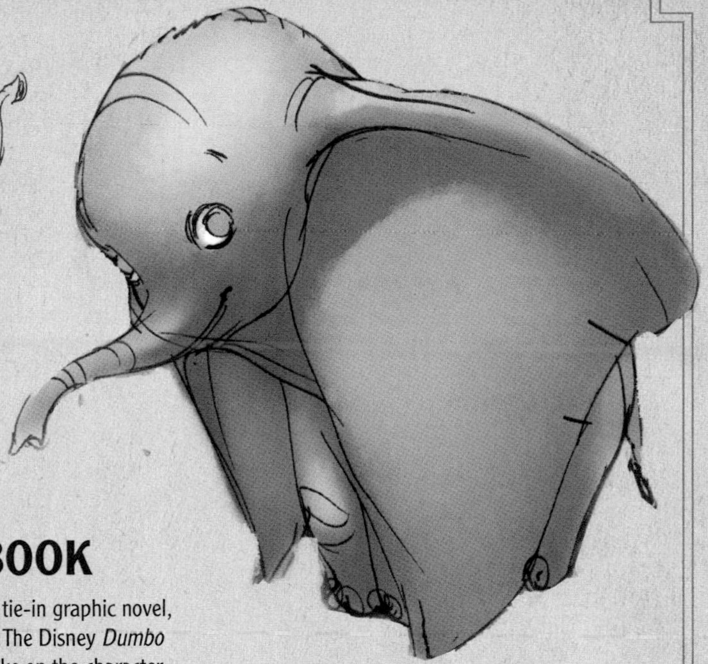

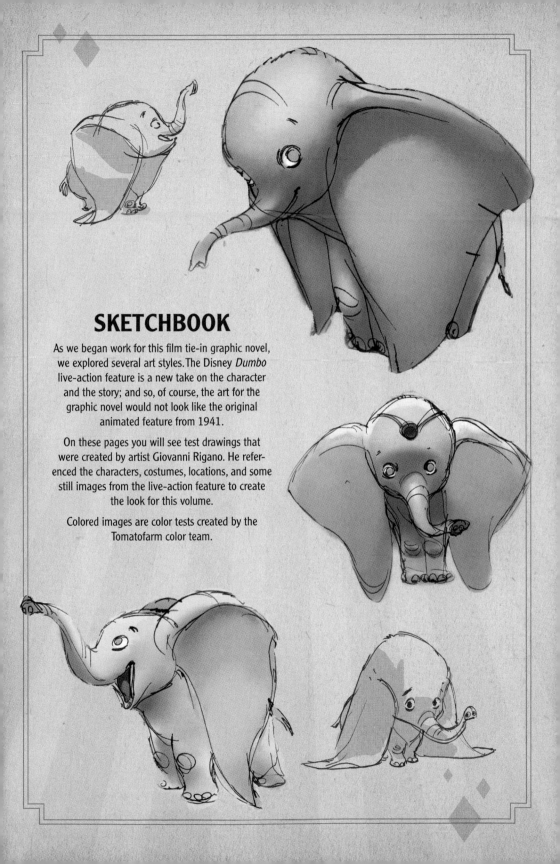

SKETCHBOOK

As we began work for this film tie-in graphic novel, we explored several art styles. The Disney *Dumbo* live-action feature is a new take on the character and the story; and so, of course, the art for the graphic novel would not look like the original animated feature from 1941.

On these pages you will see test drawings that were created by artist Giovanni Rigano. He referenced the characters, costumes, locations, and some still images from the live-action feature to create the look for this volume.

Colored images are color tests created by the Tomatofarm color team.

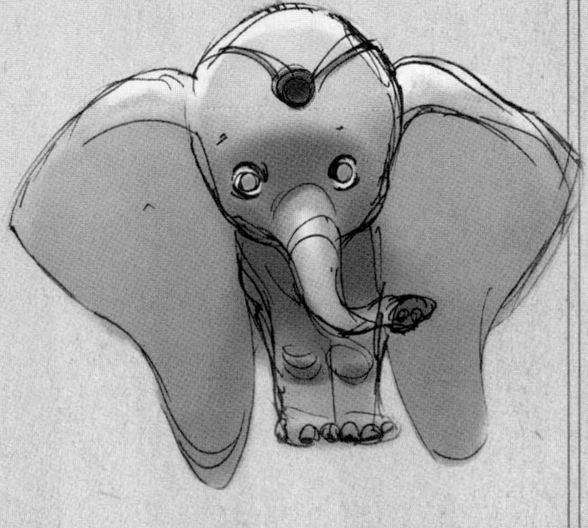

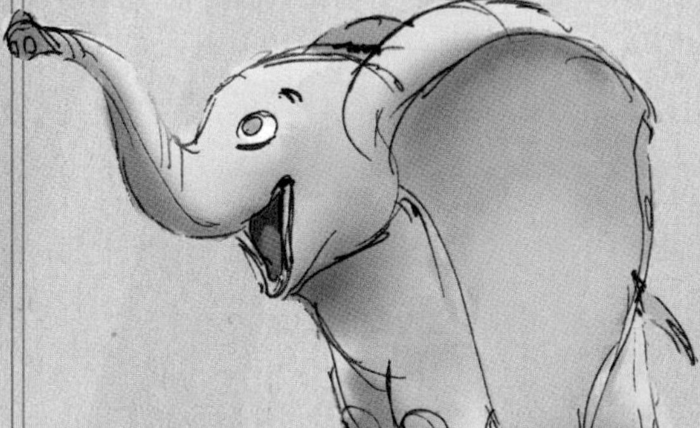

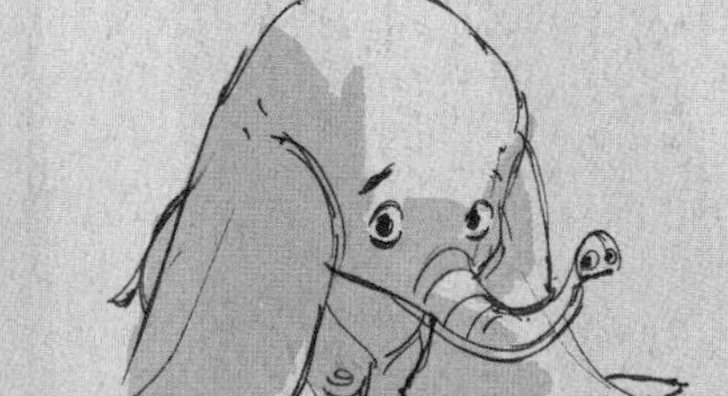

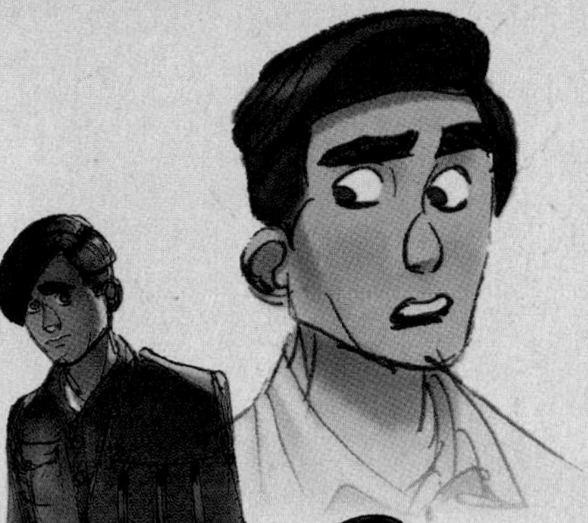

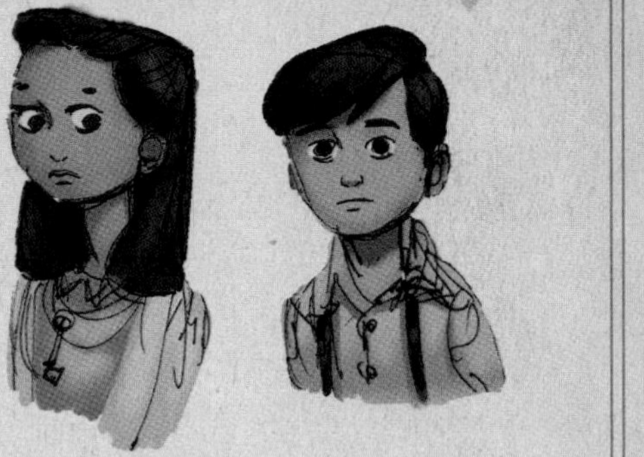

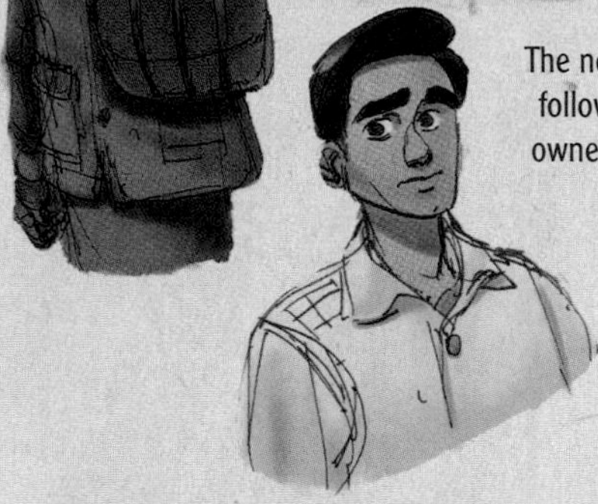

The new characters from the live-action film on these pages and the following are Holt Farrier and his children Milly and Joe, the circus owner Max Medici, and the circus performer Colette Marchant—all of whom you have met in the stories in this volume!

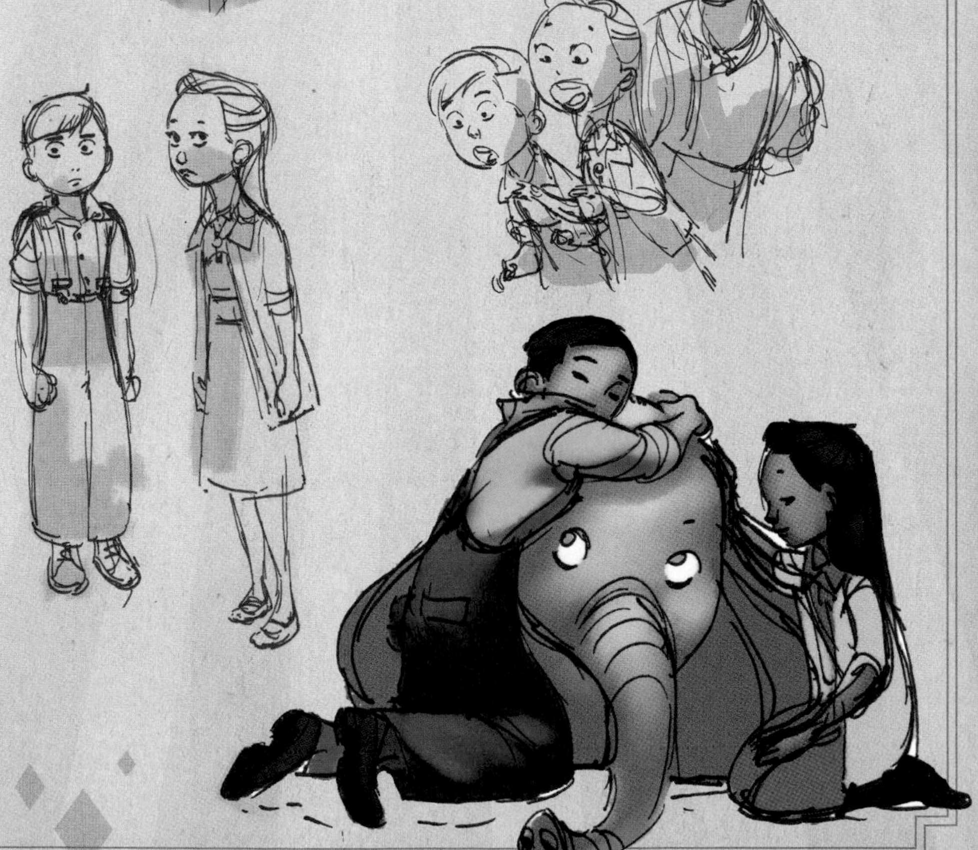

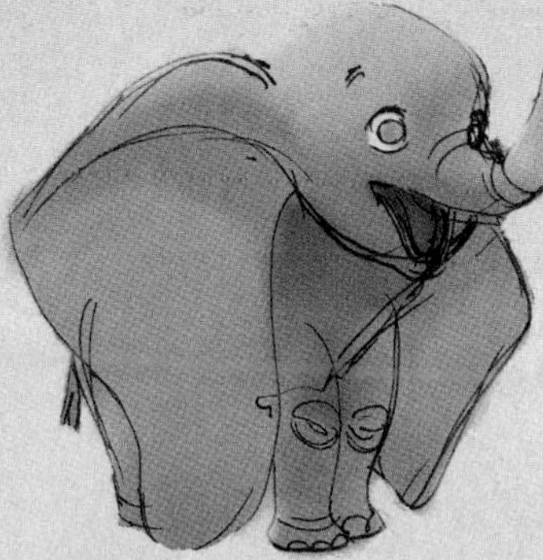

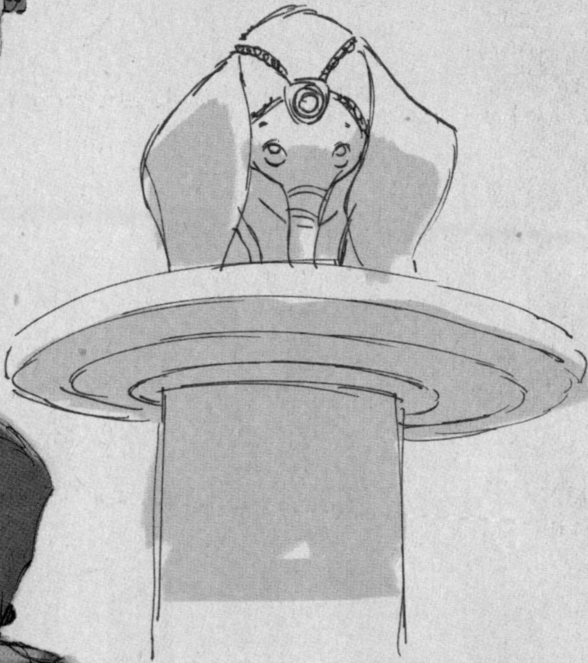

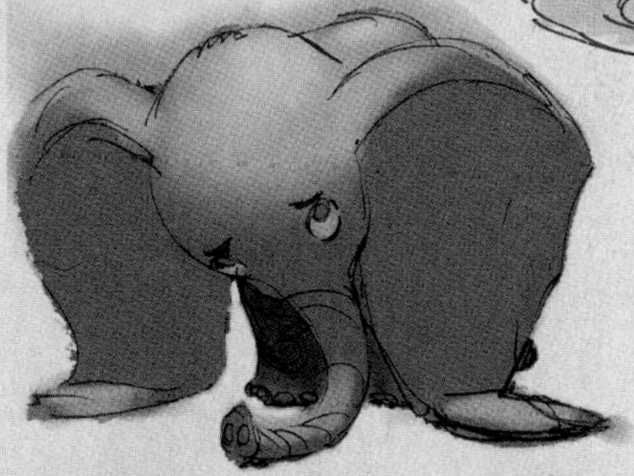

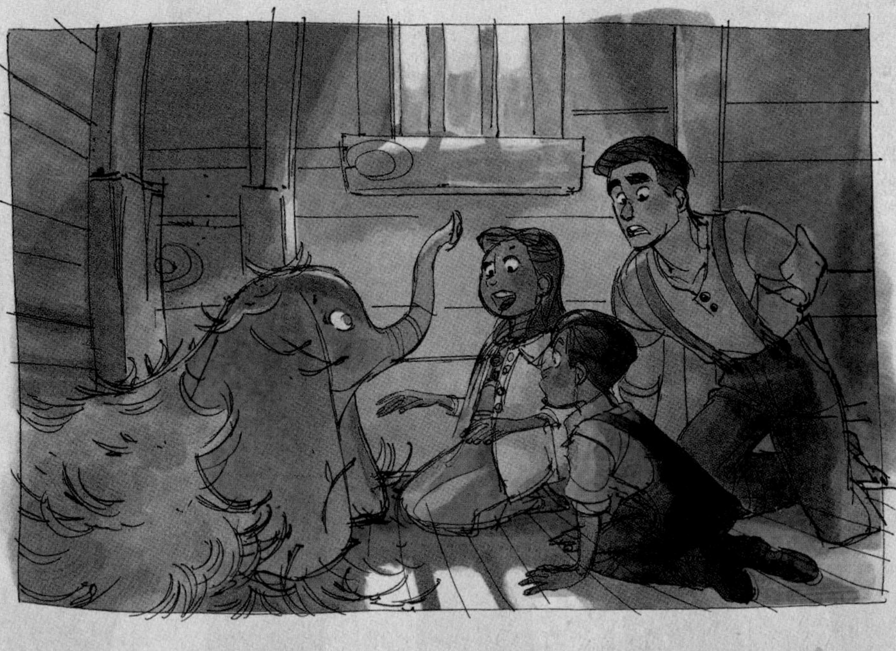

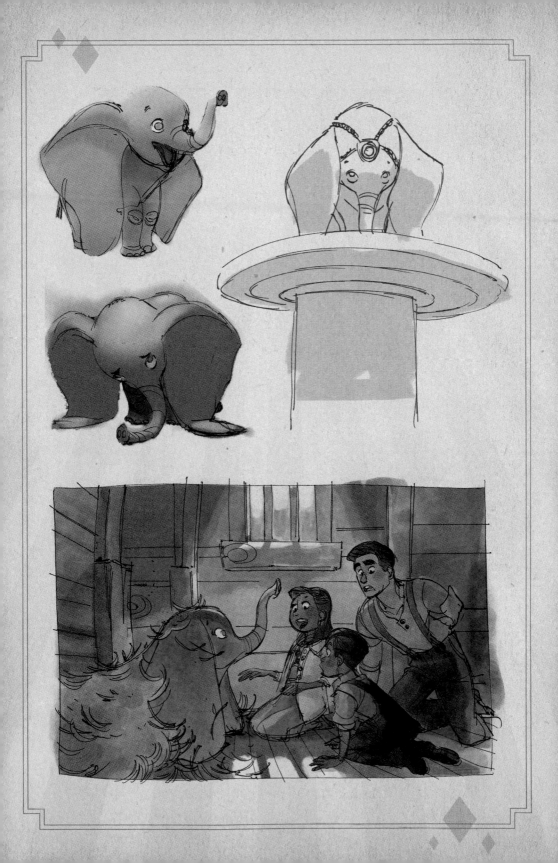

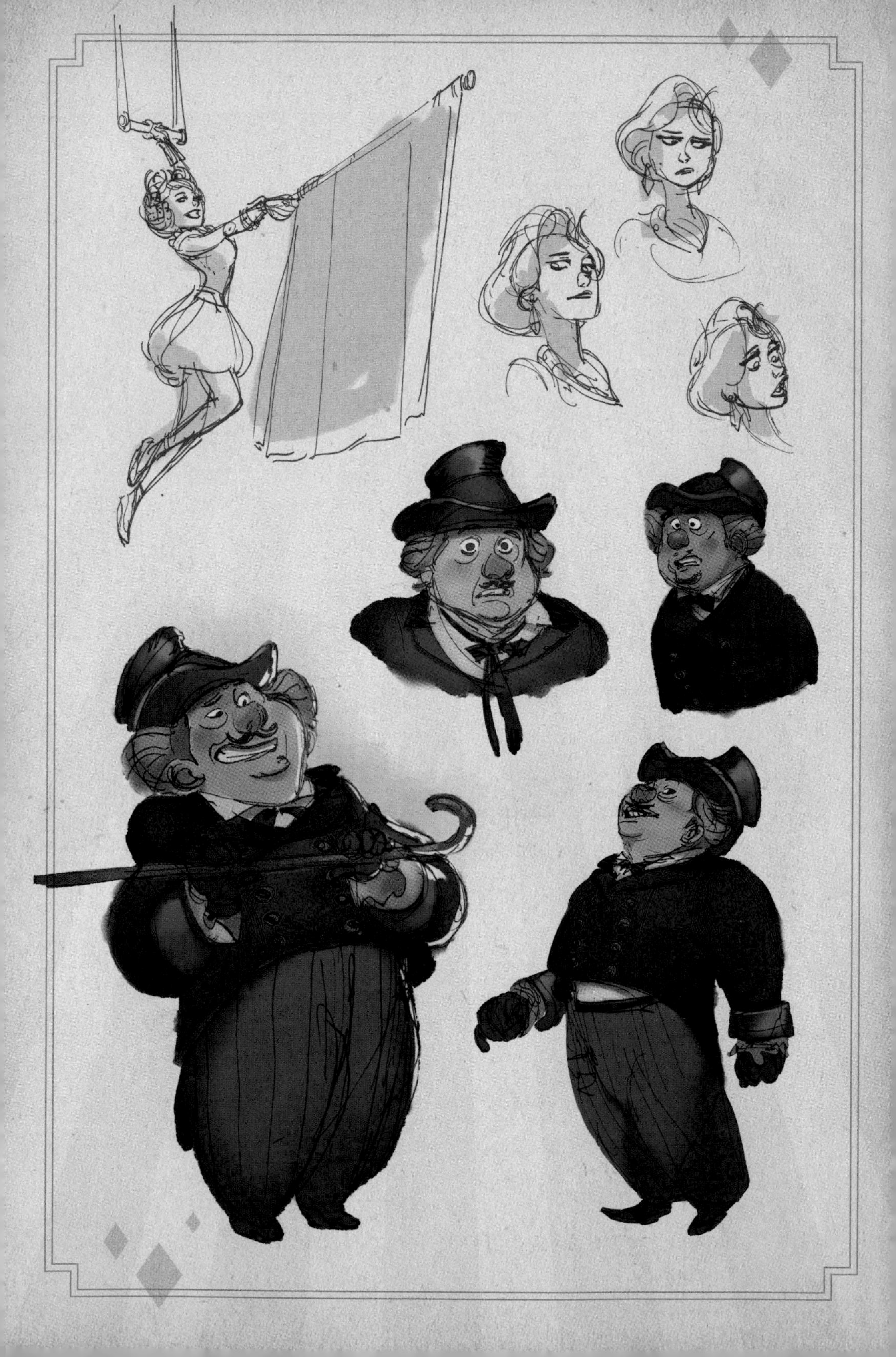